SHERLOCK HOLMES PLAYS THE GAME

BY
L F E COOMBS

Paperback ISBN 978-1-78092-729-9
ePub ISBN 978-1-78092-730-5
PDF ISBN 978-1-78092-731-2

Published in the UK by MX Publishing
335 Princess Park Manor, Royal Drive,
London, N11 3GX
www.mxpublishing.co.uk

Cover design by www.staunch.com

CONTENTS

The Lost Play
Part One: The Disturbed Tomb
Part Two: A Memorable Concert

The Dark on Dark Mystery
Part One: The Illusionist
Part Two: The Cobra

The Wrecker
An East Wind
The Devil's Tooth
The Chevereux Letter
The Barred Door Puzzle
The Whistles That Did Not Sound
The Tarrant Valley Alibi
The Electrified Canon

THE ABBEY MYSTERY
Part one: The Disturbed Tomb

In which Sherlock Holmes determines who raided a tomb in Westminster Abbey, the temporary hiding place for a William Shakespeare manuscript. The controversial 16th century play, lying among letters & tributes from friends of the deceased, contained veiled allusions to the behaviour of some who surrounded Queen Elizabeth.

Another winter morning and London's own particular fog deadened the sounds of people and vehicles in Baker Street. The fog was so thick that, as the saying goes, you could cut it with a knife. It lay thick, yellow and sulphurous, forming a thick suffocating blanket over the city. Those who ventured out had to breathe the outpourings of thousands of chimneys and the foul vapours emerging from beneath the streets. Omnibus drivers carried torches and led their horses. Hansom and growler cabmen became completely lost as once familiar streets and turnings disappeared. Distraught elderly persons clung to lampposts not daring to venture further into the unknown. The Thames was no longer a busy highway for passenger vessels and for barges and lighters. As for those with diseases of the lungs, there was no relief. They suffered dreadfully and for many the fog was the last they would ever see.

Despite all the doors being kept closed and a big bright fire in the grate the fog still managed to penetrate into our sitting room. It was with the greatest restraint on my part that I refrained from commenting on Holmes' tobacco smoke which added to the foul air. To my annoyance he seemed oblivious to my coughing and continued to puff away absorbed with some chemical problem that, to him, was far more important than fog. He had been busy with his chemical apparatus when I came down to breakfast and he gave no indication of having been to bed.

I attempted conversation by mentioning the evening violin concert for which he had tickets. He had invited me to accompany him. Not wanting to offend him I had agreed to sit for two hours listening to music the greater part of which would not be very pleasing to my ear. I have to admit to having very little understanding or knowledge concerning music as a whole and particularly pieces for the solo violin.

'Holmes, do you think this fog will prevent tonight's concert taking place? I cannot imagine how the performers will be able to find their way there.'

He did not reply immediately. He continued to peer through his microscope. Without looking up he grunted and it was a few seconds before he muttered in a voice that betrayed his annoyance at being disturbed. 'What did you say? Oh, yes, tonight's concert.' There was a long pause as he made a note of something in one of his chemical experiments notebooks. 'Have no fear on that score, Watson, artists are a very dedicated breed. It is a point of honour to never let the elements prevent them meeting an engagement. I expect we will have to walk from here.'

A walk of some distance in the foul fog was going to add to my reluctance to go out that evening.

Suddenly Holmes exclaimed, 'Watson, if I am not mistaken a cab has stopped outside our door.' A moment or two later

Superintendent Shershay of Scotland Yard entered. 'Good morning Gentlemen. Once again I come to disturb you,' was his greeting.

'Good morning,' said Holmes. 'I presume that when you come at this hour and in such dense fog the Yard needs my help and needs it without delay?'

'Just so, Mr Holmes. We have responded to a message received at dawn from the Dean of Westminster Abbey to say that one of the tombs has been disturbed and an important and ancient manuscript has been stolen. Now, please forgive my presumption, but I have a cab waiting below to convey us to the Abbey. Can you help?'

'When the Dean of the Abbey and a superintendent of the Yard together become concerned about something then it must be of some importance. Give us a moment or two and I will be ready. Oh, will you come as well, Watson?' The thought of another investigation, particularly concerning one of the noblest places in the kingdom, set aside my distaste for the fog. I agreed to accompany them.

We were soon on our way. I should mention that Shershay was a markedly different character from Inspector Lestrade. He was tall and thin. Although his manner was somewhat abrupt there could be no doubt that beneath his austere appearance he was a member of the Criminal Investigation Department who did not rush to conclusions; particularly when a suspect's future depended on justice. He was meticulous in the manner in which he gathered evidence and exhibited the utmost restraint when questioning a suspect. He never raised his fist as, I regret to have to say, other detectives were tempted to do when confronted by a stubborn villain or one who heaped abuse upon the head of the Metropolitan Police. Our lives had one thing in common because we had both served in the late Afghan War. That experience provided a basis of understanding between us.

During the general discussion of the new case taken on by my friend he said, 'Superintendent, can you tell me more about the manuscript which has been stolen?'

'All I know is what was in the Dean's brief telegram, Mr Holmes. He mentioned that the manuscript was not only of great value in monetary terms, but was of outstanding historical importance. Furthermore, its existence needs to be kept most secret. But he did not say why.'

At the lower end of Baker Street our progress became slower and slower. The fog was becoming even more dense and soon we could not see from one side of the road to the other. It took our cabman over five minutes to force his vehicle through the dense pack of carriages, omnibuses and wagons which were entangled at the crossroads in Oxford Street. We stopped and started and progressed at a walking pace through Mayfair. Crossing Trafalgar Square I observed that Nelson's statue was out of sight somewhere above the thick layer of choking fog. Despite keeping my muffler across my face, the horrible taste and smell of the fog could not be avoided. My mouth could detect the minute particles of solid matter held in suspension in the foul vapour. My nostrils were assailed by the compound of the noxious odours of the streets and the smoke from the thousands of fires that were kept stoked up to keep out the fog. I had read somewhere that if the burning of coal in household grates was prohibited then London might be spared what was in effect a self inflicted problem. My thoughts turned to the railways which formed a tangled web over the city and the hundreds of locomotives belching out smoke to add to the solid matter of the fog.

Two hours after leaving Baker Street we reached the North Transept door of the Abbey. Above us, soaring up until they were invisible in the fog, were the soot blackened ancient stones which at one time had been white. The Dean, Dr Wrestable was there to greet us and led us into the nave. The fog was thick even inside the Abbey and we could not see much further upward than the tops of the pillars which lined the nave. I thought, 'how strange that the first time I find myself in the Abbey it should be not as a member of the congregation at a service, but as part of an investigation into criminal activity.' I was certain that had the world at large known what had occurred, there would have been an outcry of rage over such desecration.

The Dean led us the down into one of the crypts. It was stygian dark and even with the lanterns carried by two constables it was difficult to discern with clarity any of the detailed features of the different tombs. We were led past a place where workmen were repairing the foundations. Their implements, wooden beams and buckets of cement took up much of the available space. The atmosphere was full of dust and everything was covered with a thick layer. In front of us was a metal grill.

'This,' said the Dean, 'was installed some time back to deter thieves from getting at the ostentatious gold ornamentation on the tomb of Roger of Aspinal. Thankfully none of the gold ornamentation or furniture has been touched. We cannot get in because who ever robbed the other tomb managed to manipulate the lock so that it cannot be opened with its key. I've sent for a locksmith. He should have arrived by now. I presume the fog is making it difficult for people to move around.'

Holmes studied the lock for a minute or two and then took from his pocket a roll of cloth and selected one of the implements which it contained. I was familiar with the set of tools which Holmes usually had with him. They enabled him to open safes, doors, padlocks and the concealed devices which locked secret drawers in desks and cabinets.

As he worked on the lock Shershay said, 'Mr Holmes I trust you do not go about after dusk carrying those tools. If a constable, who happens not to know who you are, stops you and finds them you might have some explaining to do.'

'Most unlikely that a constable would stop a gentleman,' I suggested.

'I agree, Doctor, but Mr Holmes, as we both know, sometimes disguises himself as characters likely to arouse the suspicion of a constable,' responded Shershay.

We waited and watched as different implements were applied to the lock on the gate of the grill. I began to fear that my friend had met his match. So far, none of the tools he selected could overcome the lock.

'This is certainly a cunning lock which you have had fitted, Dr Wrestable,' said Holmes. 'I should be interested to know the name of the locksmith.' He selected yet another implement. 'Well this is the last of my lock persuaders. Let us hope it is going to work.'

As he spoke, the gate swung open and he said, 'please, let me go in alone. The fewer footprints and disturbance to the scene the easier it will be for me to find clues.'

We waited while Holmes carefully examined around the tomb, on the top of which the lid had been pushed to one side. He also went into the far reaches of the crypt. When he returned he asked. 'Watson, did you bring one of the large envelopes? If so please pass it to me. I need to take away some items which could be of interest. One is this half-eaten slice of bread. It is extremely sticky. Jam of some sort.' Holmes placed what he had discovered in the envelope.

'Can we say with any certainty when the thief was down here, Superintendent?' asked Holmes.

'The crime was not discovered until eight o'clock this morning when the workmen came down to continue with restoring the foundations. They should have started work at seven but as with all of us the fog has disposed our intentions.'

'From what I have been able to observe I deduce the thief spent the whole night down here,' said Holmes, as he began to push on the lid of the tomb. 'This lid appears to be extremely heavy. Great strength would have been needed to slide it open.'

'Another thing we have to consider,' said Shershay, 'is when and how he managed to leave without anyone seeing him. Or for that matter, how did he pass through the nave, come down into the crypt and not been seen?'

'Perhaps the answer lies with the fact that he was seen,' answered Holmes. 'Observe, workmen are coming and going as we speak. Some bringing in stonework, others carrying away debris. As the Dean mentioned, some are stonemasons and others are labourers. Our thief would have been taken by the former to be a labourer and by the latter he was assumed to be a stonemason. A bag of tools is a most excellent passport. No one would have questioned his presence in the Abbey as he left by the North Transept door. And the same would apply to his arrival sometime yesterday.'

'I agree, that must have been so, Mr Holmes.'

'If you and Mr Holmes have finished,' said the Dean, 'may I get some of these men to put the lid of the tomb back?' .

They both agreed and we made our way back to the North door. As we did so Holmes asked, 'Dean, what is so important about the stolen manuscript?'

'It is a long story but I shall try and give you the essential details,' was the reply. 'Apparently, a professor at Oxford, who studies ancient documents, came upon a letter written in the hand of William Shakespeare. Without telling anyone of what he had found, he spent many hours in order to verify its authenticity. The letter was to one of Shakespeare's friends. Its importance was that it referred to a play which he had written. A play which until now was not known to exist; although many have always believed there could be plays by the Bard waiting to be discovered.'

'And, therefore, the manuscript of the play is what was taken from the tomb,' said Holmes.

'Yes,' responded the Dean. 'Some time after the death of one of Shakespeare's fellow dramatists an ornate tomb was built. Before the lid was put in place his friends put on top of his sealed lead-coffin various items, such as letters and poems in his honour. Shakespeare took the opportunity to put the manuscript of his play in the tomb. The reason for his doing so, according to the letter discovered by the professor at Oxford, was that the play contained allusions to duplicity on the part of some of those who surrounded the queen. Shakespeare feared for his life. His intention was to recover the manuscript when he was no longer in danger. However, he never did recover it and it remained forgotten until now. Although the professor and I are the only two who knew about the manuscript, I can only assume that somehow a villain found out about the letter and decided to steal the manuscript from the tomb. It is of great importance because it could settle arguments among scholars over any plays which can or cannot be attributed with certainty to Shakespeare. It is also extremely valuable.'

'What did he intend to call the play?' asked Holmes.

'Apparently it would have been *Two Queens and One Crown* referring, of course, to Elizabeth of England and Mary of Scotland,' replied the Dean. 'Shakespeare may have written something that flattered the Scottish queen or criticised Elizabeth. Or even both. They were dangerous times; even for writers.'

'I am at a loss to know how we can proceed further,' said the superintendent. 'I'll search through our records to see if anyone we have listed fits this sort of crime.'

'This is the type of crime which, in the past, I would have attributed to Professor Moriarty,' remarked, Holmes. 'Now he is no longer with us others have attempted to emulate his activities. A number of recent crimes have the hallmark of someone who is extremely cunning and who only targets the most desirable objects. Do you not agree, Shershay?'

'Certainly, Mr Holmes. Have you reached any conclusions about who the thief might be? I mean his appearance or build for example? I know you are able to describe someone from finding just one hair of their head.'

'I have. We are most likely looking for, obviously, a strong man. The lid of the tomb required the utmost effort on my part to move it. He is also not above medium height and places more weight on his left foot than on the right. He also has a front tooth missing and the middle finger of his right hand has the end missing. I venture further that he lives in Southwark or comes from somewhere near there on the south bank.'

'You seem most certain of your facts, Mr Holmes, how could you know about his missing tooth?'

'For the time being let us just say I know. I will reveal my reasons later. Now I suggest we start searching for him. London Bridge station could be a good starting point'

'I'm glad you suggest the station, Holmes,' I said. 'That part of London, apart from perhaps Waterloo station and Lambeth Palace, is not to my liking. As we all know, cabmen are none too pleased if you ask them to take you south of the river.'

When we arrived at the station Holmes said, 'Superintendent, I suggest we start at the premises of Mrs Doubleday. She makes a splendid quince and ginger conserve as well as other combinations of fruit.'

'Mr Holmes, I'm not going to question your proposal. I've worked with you for some years and gained great confidence in even the most peculiar of your proposed methods of investigation. Yes, let us proceed.'

Our cabman was finding it difficult to find his way to the address Holmes gave him. He called down from his box, 'don't come this side of the river much. I can finds me way anywhere on t'other side. This blinking fog ain't helping.'

After a tortuous journey in the thick fog among one of the less savoury parts of London we arrived at Mrs Doubleday's premises. Inside we found ourselves wreathed in clouds of hot steam from the many vats of bubbling fruit which surrounded us. Mrs Doubleday, who presided over the steam equivalent of an inferno, was figuratively and physically a tower of strength. Her stentorian voice gave orders to her minions as they laboured to produce some of the finest marmalades, jams and other preserves to be found in the kingdom. I was appalled at the conditions in which the many young girls were having to work and in particular their rather indelicate lack of clothing. Some of them were employed in crushing fruit with their bare feet as they stood in large wooden troughs. The stone floor was slippery with crushed fruit of various kinds. I presumed the only advantage to the girls of such employment was the readily available wholesome diet of fruit.

Shouting to make himself heard, Holmes said, 'Mrs Doubleday, you make a wonderful quince and ginger preserve. May I ask, do you sell much of it to the people of Southwark?'

'I'm afraid it's too expensive for the likes of them what lives round 'ere. Mind you there's one cove what always 'as much of the ready, who sometimes buys a jar.'

'His name, if you please?'

'No idea. Queer sort a chap. Don't think 'e comes from rand 'ere. Even 'as a sovereign with 'im to pay. Don't see many of them on a bloke like im.'

'Was he a strong looking man with one front tooth missing?'

'Well, yus. He's a 'orrible grin and big stickin' art teeth an' wun's missing.'

'Madam, you have been most helpful. Thank you,' said Holmes as we left.

'Mr Holmes,' said Shershay, 'I would rather not start looking for him round here until I've called at the local station and let the superintendent there know what I am doing in his area. It is, after all, a matter of politeness. Another reason is to seek some help from constables who normally patrol this part of London and are well acquainted with the local villianary.'

The result of our visit to the local police station was to be told that a suspicious character answering Holmes' description had sometimes been seen but he had never been arrested. Our party was reinforced by two of the largest constables I had ever come across. They were known both within the force and by the public as Gog and Magog; the legendary giants whose effigies guard the Mansion House. Their size, or rather their bulk, was most reassuring as we started to penetrate the narrow, twisting streets and the jumble of ancient structures which lined the river bank. This bank of the river had not been improved in appearance, as the opposite bank had, by a proper stone embankment and roadway. The fog continued to hamper our search. At the sight of the two giants the way before us became devoid of people. I will not dwell on the methods employed by the two officers of the law to extract information from one or two of the villainous characters encountered. Their far from delicate questioning of one of them produced a result. When he was brought before us, held firmly by one ear, he said, 'Ow, ow, yer hurtin' me.' Another twist of the ear and, 'orl right, lay of, that bloke's dun me no fafor. He's in the Spindlers Street werharse.' Within a few seconds of his ear being released he had disappeared from our sight. By then the fog was becoming more intense and we could not see further than about five yards in front.

'What is our next move?' asked Holmes.

One of the constables replied, 'we've got to move carefully, Sir. If he hears us coming he'll make a bolt for it and jump into a boat and as it is close to high tide he'll be swept away from us and be well upstream.'

'Superintendent, the constable is right. It is most important that we lay our hands on him in order to learn where the manuscript is or, more than likely, the name of the master mind who is waiting for it.'

As we approached the warehouse, as silently as we could, I mused, 'once again I find myself being led into a dangerous situation. What if the one we seek has others with him? What if they are armed? I recalled standing on a rocky outcrop in Afghanistan with bullets whistling around me and not being too concerned. But, then, I was younger. Getting older does not necessarily endow one with greater courage.'

Much to my relief, but to the annoyance of Holmes and Shershay, there was no sign of our quarry. We did find, however, at the back of the warehouse a partly concealed door which led into a small covered dock. The iron bar gate at the end, leading to the river, was open.

A search of the dock was started. Nothing much of interest was found until Holmes said, 'Superintendent, this pile of coal and this can of oil suggest that a steam launch is kept here. This may be how he's slipped our grasp. If he still has the manuscript with him he is now on his way to deliver it to who paid him to steal it.'

'My mistake, Mr Holmes,' admitted Shershay. 'I should have alerted the Thames Division to keep watch from the river. If he's used the launch then he's well away.'

'However, he may not have used the launch. There is no smell of the smoke or hot steam and oil which would indicate that it had been in here recently. No, perhaps more likely he used a rowing boat and has taken advantage of the flow of the river to move quickly upstream.'

'I agree, Mr Holmes,' responded the superintendent. 'We are now faced with the problem of where to start looking for him.'

'Superintendent, he may have only gone a short distance up stream and then stepped ashore on either bank. This thick fog will hide his movements.'

The onset of night and the fog forced us to abandon the search for the day. We returned to Baker Street. Had the cabman not been ordered to wait we would have found ourselves stranded in a part of London where cabs were few and far between; particularly in thick fog.

Not until the next morning was the subject of the Abbey affair raised again. 'Did you have any thoughts in the night, Holmes, about where the Abbey thief went?' I enquired.

'None what so ever, my dear chap. I have dismissed the whole affair from my thoughts. I find that it pays to leave a problem for a day or two and then come back to it with the mind refreshed. Often, that produces an answer. In the meantime I have been requested to scrutinise a doctoral dissertation which has been submitted on the subject of the criminal mind. I will now first reinforce my faculties with this exceptionally strong and aromatic tobacco that one my clients sent me, and concentrate on what is before me.'

I busied myself with working from notes I had made of a recent investigation conducted successfully by my friend. I realised that there was ample material in front of me from which to write, what I anticipated, could be an absorbing tale. In doing so I had to keep in mind Holmes' strictures concerning including too much sensational writing. He often commented on my efforts to do justice to his skill. 'It was more luck than judgement, Watson. I did not have to apply too much reasoning'; or, 'yes, it was a struggle but he was no match for some of the special tricks I possess and it was all over within a few seconds.'

Now and then muffled exclamations would emerge from the cloud of smoke surrounding his favourite chair; such as, 'pretentious rubbish,' 'not so, definitely not so,' 'who is this chap, Fraud?'

Another day passed and Holmes did not mention the missing play. Only after he had been immersed in his commonplace books for some time did the subject once again come to my attention. 'Listen to this, Watson, I read from an old cutting that there are a number of prominent collectors of ancient books and manuscripts who have always gone to great lengths to acquire a particular one. This suggests that, instead of trying to find the villain who desecrated the tomb in the Abbey, I should concentrate on those who would prize it for their collection.'

'That will certainly reduce the number of suspects. Does the cutting give any names that are familiar?'

'One or two. A singular fact is the presence in this particular corner of the collectors' market of the Brothers Trawton. Apparently, they are bitter rivals when it comes to ancient documents and manuscripts. The elder, Thomas, was willing to provide the magazine, which had published the article I had kept, with as much information as they wanted; including a photograph. Whereas, although the author of the article does not say so directly, the other brother, Arthur, was unwilling to talk to journalists. All that could be reported about him was what little information his brother was able to provide.'

'From what you are saying, Holmes, I assume the other collectors mentioned have been dismissed from your inquiry?'

'For the time being, yes. Of course, Arthur Trawton may have nothing to do with the stolen play yet something tells me, intuition perhaps, I should first attempt to eliminate him from the list before examining the remaining collectors.'

'Where does he live?'

Holmes studied the article and replied, 'both brothers live within a short distance of each other in Streatham. What I need to do now is somehow to bait my line, as it were, to see if Arthur Trawton rises to it.'

'How will you do that?'

'Well, as you know, I always endeavour to read the small private notices that are printed in the newspapers. They contain far more information than might be expected by a brief glance of just one or two lines. I will insert one in the principal papers which, I hope, will bring he who holds Shakespeare's lost play to the surface. It could be Trawton or even someone of whom I have never heard.'

'How will you word it?'

'Perhaps as follows: "There is a companion to the missing Avon play. Reply post restant, Strand P.O. Hathaway".'

'How long before you go to the post office in the Strand?'

'If the one who has the play reads it he will respond within a day I imagine. Let us say three days from now.'

Not until the third visit to the post office was a letter awaiting Holmes. After reading it Holmes said, 'Watson, the writer of this, who gives no name, proposes that we meet alongside Cleopatra's Needle on the Embankment at ten of the evening of next Thursday.'

'Shall I come with you? Much devilry could be afoot.'

'Indeed, my dear fellow. Your presence would be most reassuring. However, keep some distance away otherwise who ever I am to meet might become suspicious. I'm certain he assumes that I am a criminal who has acquired by dubious means another missing play.'

'I presume I will have to be in disguise?'

'If you do not mind. May I propose that you don some disreputable garments from my collection and with a bottle, on a piece of string tied round your waist, you slump on the pavement apparently at peace with the world and the contents of the bottle? Mind you, if a constable should come along do not let him find your revolver. You would then have some difficult explaining to do.'

'Oh,' I exclaimed, 'I must take my revolver then?'

'To be on the safe side. Although I anticipate that there will be no rough stuff.'

'I hope you are proved right.'

The appointment was kept. I played my part to the best of my ability. I sat with my back to the parapet and adopted a slumped inebriated posture. The only thing that was out of concert with my disguise was the cleanliness of my attire. The clothes were indeed ragged and patched and exhibited many different hues but they had obviously been laundered by Mrs Hudson. Had anyone come close to me then they would be surprised at the lack of the expected unpleasant odours.

Holmes had only been standing close to the Needle for a minute or two when a portly man, who's Ulster did not disguise his significant girth, ambled past without stopping. Another minute passed and the same man came walking back. This time he stopped in front of Holmes.

Apart from the shaking of heads and gesticulations of hands and arms, nothing untoward happened. I could not hear what was being said. Holmes had disguised his features and the one he met kept his face covered. After the short meeting we returned to Baker Street. On the way Holmes told me what had happened.

'I was not surprised to be told that I was meeting an emissary of the unknown collector. I was questioned about the provenance of the play and what sum was being asked. I have to admit I was on dangerous ground. I had to bluff my way along. I implied that I could provide proof of the provenance of the play I was willing to sell but I would not deal through a middleman. It was agreed that a time and place would be announced in the Times next Monday. It was anticipated that such a step would lead to a meeting with the collector himself.'

'My dear fellow, you have placed yourself in an impossible situation. How can you provide proof?'

'I will provide some manuscript pages that may have been part of another recently discovered Shakespeare play of very doubtful provenance. The professor at Oxford, I am sure, will allow me to hand over a copy. That should be sufficient to convince the collector that I hold a complete play and that further negotiations can take place leading to the moment when I hand over some ancient but worthless paper and I find out with whom I am dealing.'

'Are you not going to pursue the villain who actually stole the play from the Abbey?'

'For the time being, I am concentrating on Streatham and not the Thames'.

Each day we carefully read all the notices in the Times.

'At last,' exclaimed Holmes, 'here it is. It says "Hathaway meet at the Café Royal bring the collector at 9 am on 20th."'

'Who is the collector,' I asked.

'Not who, dear fellow, but what. He means the magazine read by antiquarians.'

'When you meet I expect he will be disguised as I am sure you will be. Of course, you will be able to apply your customary scrutiny of his manner and dress from which you will gather enough information from which to establish his identity.'

'That is my intention'

'What of the valuable manuscript you are using as bait?'

'The answer, Watson, should arrive soon.'

He was right. A little later two large young men entered the sitting room. From their dress I deduced, or attempted to deduce, that they were university men.

'May I introduce these two gentlemen from Oxford,' said Holmes. 'Their tutor is the professor who discovered the missing play.'

After the introductions a cloth was unrolled to reveal some obviously ancient sheets of paper. 'These are assumed to be part of the manuscript of another lost Shakespearean play,' explained Holmes.

'They are in his actual hand?'

'Unfortunately not. If they were their value would be astounding. As we know, little of the Bard's actual writing has survived. These were more than likely written by one of the players at the Globe Theatre copying from the original. I am inclined to think they are cunning forgeries. Of course, I could be wrong and they might be very valuable.'

'But, surely, if they are, they must not be allowed to be used for what you intend?'

'Certainly not. I will accompany these gentlemen and the papers to the offices of the Strand magazine. There they have a wonderful photographic apparatus that will provide us with fac-similes. These originals will then return to Oxford in the custody of these two rugby Blues.'

Carrying a copy of the *Collector* Holmes kept the appointment at the Café Royal. On his return he said, 'I am now certain it was Arthur Trawton who was having breakfast when I arrived at the Café Royal. Neither of us attempted an introduction by name. I passed over the photographic fac-similes. I said little. The fewer words exchanged the better in order not to reveal who I was, lest my simple disguise was not sufficient to hide my identity. We agreed a further meeting would take place at which I would hand over the complete play in exchange for ten thousand pounds.'

'That's a vast unbelievable sum.'

'Watson, I have no idea whether, in the criminal world, that is or is not the market price.'

'You say you are certain you met Arthur Trawton?'

'In the first place, his false side whiskers were not properly attached. I have trained myself to study faces and to see through any additions; such as whiskers and beards. Secondly, I realised that the dish of conserve he had ordered with his toast and coffee was quince and ginger. Furthermore he had forgotten that his cuff links were engraved with an A and a T.

'Oh, I see. The thief in the Abbey was partial to such a conserve and you think there is a connection between the two men.'

'Yes, I do. The thief is more than likely in his employ.'

'Once again, my dear chap, you have reached an important conclusion in a case. All that needs to be done is for Shershay and his men to go to Arthur Trawton's house and recover the stolen play.'

'Not so fast, Watson. It will require more than my observation of the initials on a pair of cuff links. There may be more than one collector with similar cuff links and engraved initials whose methods are far from ethical. No, we need to study Arthur Trawton's mansion in Streatham from a distance before taking any positive action.'

We took a cab to Streatham. After a number of years accompanying my friend during his detective ventures I had become accustomed to his careful questioning of local shopkeepers and tradesmen in order to establish the habits, preferences and standing of the inhabitants of a particular house. One of the questions was, of course, 'do you supply quince and ginger conserve to any of the houses around here?' To my surprise none of the grocers did so.

'It appears that AT of Streatham is not our man,' said I.

'Not necessarily so, Watson. One of his servants could fetch it from the conserves factory in Southwark, and that person could also be the thief. Our next move has to be a close inspection of his house and grounds.'

Leaving our cab round the corner, so as not to let the cabman know where we were going, we studied the well laid out grounds surrounding a large Italianate style house in one of the most desirable roads in Streatham Hill. Outwardly it appeared what it intended to present. Namely, the home of one of the many prosperous merchants who chose that part of London to live in sylvan surroundings; yet only twenty minutes or so by train from their businesses in the West End or the City.

'Well tended lawns,' commented Holmes.

From behind some trees came the sight and sound of a lawn mowing machine being pushed by a stocky well-built gardener. When he came close to the railings Holmes called to him. 'Good morning my man. Please will you direct us to the Laurels? I believe we have come too far.'

The gardener replied in monosyllabic grunts and pointed back down the way we had come.'

'Thank you, good day,' said Holmes. We moved away.

'Got him!' exclaimed Holmes. 'The end of the middle finger of his right-hand is missing. Arthur Trawton's gardener is the one who stole the play.'

We regained our cab and at the first post office we came to Holmes dispatched a telegram to Shershay. That evening we accompanied the superintendent to Trawton's house. The door was not immediately opened in response to the ringing of the bell and the shout of 'Police, open the door.' We could hear voices raised in anger and then silence followed by the door being opened. The house was full of priceless objects d'art and antiques, including paintings, many of which matched descriptions in the lists of stolen goods which the

26

superintendent had brought with him. Trawton was arrested and taken away.

On our way back to Baker Street I commented, 'I noticed, Holmes, that when we were in Trawton's house you picked up a cigar end.'

'It is the remains of an Indian cheroot. I observed that Trawton did not smoke. There were no receptacles in his study for ash other than the hearth. He had had a visitor just before we arrived who must have left quickly from the back of the house. When I have the time I will analyse the remains of the cheroot and determine its exact type and that might lead us to who the visitor was.'

'You suspect he is an accomplice of Trawton?'

'Possibly. When he heard the police were at the door he must have made off through the garden at the back because he did not want to become involved.'

Reading the paper next morning I learned how Superintendent Shershay of Scotland Yard had successfully tracked down and recovered priceless antiques which had been stolen over a number of years. The paper gave much space to the wickedness and deceit of someone who had been accepted in the highest circles of society as an authority on antiquities and as an honest dealer.

'No mention of your part in all this, Holmes. Only Shershay's name is given. You deserve greater recognition.'

'Perhaps. But the other side of the coin is my wish to remain, as it were, in the shadows. Too much exposure in the press could alert the world of the criminals and inhibit those occasions when I have to enter it in pursuit of information. For much of my time I play the game for the sake of the game.'

Oh, come to think of it, how were you able to deduce so much about the thief; the missing tooth, for example?'

'Simple, my dear fellow, the half eaten piece of bread I found. I could clearly see from the impression made by his teeth that one was missing.'

'And the finger?'

'He had left behind a bottle of ale on which there was a clear impression of his right hand fingers in the dust and spilt ale.'

'His height?'

'At first I found it difficult to deduce his height. However, I happened to look above my head at the vaulting, which came down low above the tomb, and could see that the dust and cobwebs had not been disturbed. A tall man would have touched the vaulting with the top of his head.'

'One thing in particular, Holmes, that surprised me during this investigation, was when you referred to intuition. Surely, you have frequently impressed upon me that intuition should not be part of scientific detection.'

'Quite right. Intuition is unscientific.'

'I presume that you observed his footprints in the dust and were able to deduce he had a limp.'

'Quite so. Altogether my deductions were really rather basic detective work; nothing more. Now, if you do not mind, dear

28

fellow I must concentrate on determining to which of a number of brands or types this fragment of cheroot belongs.

NOTES

That part of London stretching close along the right-bank of the Thames, from about Chelsea Bridge to Woolwich, was not developed to the same extent as on the left-bank. There were fewer noble buildings and sumptuous houses. Between the thoroughfares that radiated from the bridges the streets and alleyways were lined with mean houses, hovels and warehouses as well as manufactories and wharves.

Part Two: A Memorable Concert

In which Holmes is kidnapped and held for ransom.

Although the ancient manuscript had been found it was not the end of the affair either for Holmes or myself. A few days later I was in the consulting room of the doctor with whom I had once shared a practice. Occasionally I acted as his locum.

It was just as I was about to leave for the day when two men pushed their way into the surgery. One held a revolver and announced, 'forgive our unseemly arrival, Dr Watson.'

'Who are you? What do you want? If it is money you will be disappointed.' Was all I could think of saying.

'Not money Doctor,' said one of them. 'We want some of your blood.'

'Why should they want my blood?' I realised I was in great danger. 'Should I attempt to resist?' was my first thought. But the sight of the pistol close to my face put paid to any such idea. I said, as calmly as I could, 'I do not understand why you want my blood'

'If you do exactly as we ask we will only need a few drops,' was the reply. 'Please sit at your desk.'

I sat down wondering what they were going to do.

'Now take one of your prescription forms and write as I dictate,' said the one who obviously was in command.

I had to write: *Mr Holmes, go with the gentlemen to each side of you. Do not shout or struggle otherwise your friend will suffer.*

They looked at what I had been forced to write. 'Good,' said the larger of the two intruders. 'Now prick your thumb and smear blood on what you have written.'

I did so.

'One of your visiting cards please, Doctor.'

I handed one over and it was pocketed along with my short note. At that they left, leaving me relieved but confused. 'Why, why get me to write those words and why smear them with my blood. Why demand my card?' Those thoughts filled my head. A glass of brandy helped to steady my nerves. 'Come on Watson,' I said to myself. 'Think hard about what has happened. Could it be they intend to force Holmes to divulge information or, as the note indicated, to go with them? My blood on the note is intended, perhaps, to persuade him I am being harmed.'

I realised that I had to act immediately. My friend could be in great danger. I hastened to 221B Baker Street. My first words to Mrs Hudson were, 'Mr Holmes. Is he here?'

'No, Doctor, he's gone to a concert. He's there now.'

'Which concert, where?'

'I'm sorry, he did not say. I was not here when he left. I'd put out his evening clothes this morning and he only said he was going to a concert, but not which one.'

Frantically I scanned the advertisements in the newspapers hoping to determine where Holmes was. There were three concerts of the type he favoured. I would have to go to all three.

'Get the boy to fetch a cab, please Mrs Hudson. 'There is no time to be lost.'

The cab took me to all three in turn. At the third the manager told me, in reply to my question about my friend, that of course he knew him. He had been there but left during the interval with two gentlemen. The manager was surprised because he knew Holmes was a great admirer of Sarasate's violin playing. I could have kicked myself for not remembering Holmes' fondness for Sarasate. Had I done so I would have been able to act more quickly.

Obviously, Holmes had been taken away and had not resisted because of what I had been forced to write. I was ashamed of my weakness. I had led my friend into a trap. All I could do now was inform Superintendent Shershay of the Yard and Holmes' brother Mycroft. Telegrams were duly sent explaining what had occurred and what I feared. As I thought about what had happened I came to realise that I had failed to observe anything that would distinguish those who had made me act as I did. I anticipated that Holmes would make some cutting comments on my failure. Had he been in my place, no doubt, he would, from their manner of speaking and their clothes, have determined much about them.

Shershay and Mycroft Holmes came round as soon as they could and we discussed what we assumed could be the kidnapping of my friend. Unfortunately, as they explained, there was little to go on and although an immediate inquiry would be made among the many police informers, we could only await the arrival of a ransom demand. However, I expected that Mycroft Holmes would use his unique position in Whitehall to help. All important decisions taken by certain government departments were passed to him for an opinion before they were acted upon. From time to time Holmes had asked for his brother's help and invariably the advice and opinions had enabled him to resolve successfully a convoluted problem.

For two days nothing was heard of the missing foremost detective in the kingdom and then in the evening of the second I heard the front door open, footsteps coming up the stairs, the door opened and there was Holmes.

I hid my heartfelt relief at seeing him by limiting my emotions 'Ah, it's you Holmes, Where have you been?'

'Before I tell you of my adventure I must know if the villains harmed you?'

'Not at all but, more importantly, how are you feeling and what on earth happened to you? I regret very much in giving way to their threats and having to write a note that I knew could lead you into danger.'

'My dear friend, you could do nothing else. I will endeavour to recount all that occurred over the past two days, but I think I need a whisky and soda and then a bath.'

'Take your time, dear fellow. I will send telegrams immediately to your brother and Shershay.'

I could tell there was something wrong with him. Not physical but possibly mental. Despite my insistence that perhaps, after all, he should delay going over the events of the past two days and leave it until he was sufficiently recovered, he insisted on recounting what had happened. 'I need to tell you now before I forget some important detail. I should be most grateful if you were to take a few notes, Watson.'

'Certainly, Holmes. I'm ready.'

He curled up in his favourite chair, drank a glass of whisky and soda, lit a pipe and started the account of his adventure.

'It all started with a brandy at the bar of the concert hall during the interval. I was hardly aware of the men standing at the side of me because my thoughts were on music and the forthcoming recital after the interval by Sarasate. A voice interrupted my thoughts with, "good evening, Mr Holmes, please read this." A piece of paper was handed to me. Well you know what was written on it.'

'I do indeed, my dear friend. I must repeat, I bitterly regret having led you into a trap.'

'No, please do not blame yourself. What else could you have done?'

'My blood on my words, I presume, led you to believe they were harming me.'

'Yes. The sight of your card and the instructions was enough to convince me I should go with them. I was taken in a cab down to the landing stage at Westminster and onto a steam launch. Once on board a hood was placed over my head and the launch got under weigh.'

'Can you recall how far they took you?'

'I regret, my dear fellow, I could gain no information from what I could hear other than, as I said, I was being taken in a steam-powered vessel. After, I suppose, about an hour I sensed we were alongside the river bank. Still hooded, I was led off the launch and forced to stumble up some steps. At the top of the steps I could tell I was in a house. After going up some stairs I was pushed into a chair to which I was bound by cords.

'You had no idea of where you were?'

'None, but that did not concern me at the time because when the hood was whipped off there, staring me in the face, was that villain Tresscot-Jones.'

'Not he of the Deerstalker affair, surely not?'

'Yes, that is he. The companion at the time of the late unlamented Moriarty. "Welcome, Mr Holmes," he said, with an icy intonation. "I'm so pleased you have arrived safely. I must apologise for any discomfort during the journey. I can see you are somewhat surprised to see me. You not only caused the death of my companion Professor Moriarty but you interfered in our attempt to seize the Boswell Concentrator". As he spoke I began to learn that he claimed to have taken the place of Moriarty in the criminal world. He began to boast about his exploits and in doing so provided the answers to a number of unsolved crimes in the records of the Criminal Investigation Department at Scotland Yard; including one or two in which I had been part of the investigation. His gloating manner and obvious delight at having captured me made me fume with rage. Had I been free I would gladly have throttled him. As it was, all I could do was listen. At the end of a monologue of criminal activities he said, "I expect, my dear Mr Holmes, you anticipate being held and only released on payment of a ransom. As you are who you are, that would be a considerable sum. No, that is not the purpose of your visit to my house". I responded. "So Tresscot-Jones what is your intention?".'

'He told me he had learned that I was writing a book on the detection of crime. Furthermore, Scotland Yard and other police forces had encouraged the enterprise and that it would become required reading for all amateur and professional detectives. However, his informants had discovered that I had decided against publishing. He much regretted my decision as he would have found the book most valuable as he would have been able take steps to avoid any of his activities inadvertently being exposed or frustrated.'

'I replied, "I apologise for disappointing you. I abandoned the writing of such a book for the good reason, as you have mentioned, that criminals like you, for example, would benefit from its advice. For example, in your case, you left the end of your cheroot in Trawton's house. I was able to match it to one of the many specimens of tobacco and ash that I have gathered and labelled. It did not take me long to determine that it was you who scurried out of the back when Trawton's house was raided by the police".'

'He continued: "The decision not to publish is why you are here. It is still my intention to acquire your knowledge. I intend to extract from your mind all that you intended to include in the book; particularly relating to advice on how to frustrate my work".'

' "Torture is a cowardly act; particularly by one who affects the manners of a gentleman," was my reply.'

"Thank you for the compliment, Mr Holmes. However the tone of your voice leads me to believe you do not consider me to be a gentleman. No, I am not going to subject you to physical torture. I have a far more subtle way of extracting what I need to know."

'As he spoke, I confess I was inwardly afraid, Watson. Even more so when he produced a hypodermic syringe and started to fill it.'

' "This should do the trick. This is a drug which I discovered in India. It releases your mind so effectively that any questions put to you under its influence will be answered without hesitation and with complete honesty." He sneered. "I understand you are no stranger to drugs capable of inducing unusual states of mind".'

'At that he injected me in the arm. Within about a minute I became only aware that my mind was no longer within my head. It also seemed as if I was outside my own body and watching it from a distance.'

'My dear fellow that was a despicable act. Did the effects of the drug last for long?'

'I cannot say with certainty. The next day the effects had diminished. That night, the second, I was once again in a small steam launch with a hood over my head. I was reminded that your fate was in my hands and therefore I should make no attempt to escape or call for help. After what may have been an hour we bumped against a mooring and the hood was removed. I was taken ashore and pushed into a waiting cab. The two masked men who sat with me said nothing. I could see some familiar streets and places and then, to my surprise, we were in Baker Street. I was pushed out onto the pavement and the cab raced away. In front of me was our doorway. The rest you know.'

'A terrible experience for you, my dear friend. I suppose the important question is did Tresscot-Jones succeed in extracting information from you?'

'I wish I knew the answer. Far more important is the need to find the villain as quickly as possible. At this actual moment he could be perusing the notes I presume he took of what I was forced to reveal.'

When Shershay and Mycroft arrived the next morning we sat down to plan a concerted attempt to find Tresscot-Jones.

'If we are to find where you were held prisoner, we need to apply the method you told me about and have used on a number of occasions,' suggested the superintendent. 'That is you will have to try and recall, step by step, the journey and the sights, sounds and smells as well as what you can recall about the house in which you were held.'

'I agree, Superintendent. Therefore, for the account of what happened to me I will start with the journey in the steam launch. I am certain we moved upstream. I say upstream because had we gone downstream we would quickly have been among the mass of barges and ships that crowd the Pool of London. The noise of tugs, ships, stevedores, lightermen and all the other activities of a port could not have been mistaken.'

'Yes, upstream was more than likely,' said Mycroft Holmes.

Holmes continued his recollection of the journey. 'At one point I could hear the distinctive chiming of the clock on the tower of Saint Simions church near Chelsea Reach. As we progressed the noises associated with the Thames began to lessen. I did not have the wit to count the bridges as we passed under them. The sound made by the launch echoed back from the underside of each bridge.'

'Were you aware of how many were with you in the launch?' I asked.

'More than one, Watson, because, after about an hour, someone said, "will we make it? The tide's right out. Is there enough water?" Soon after we stopped I was half carried off the launch, pushed up some steps and a flight of stairs. The hood was removed and I was confronted by Tresscot-Jones.'

'You say that after you had been subjected to the drug they left you to recover. Were you able to work out what type of house you were in?' asked Shershay.

'The room was in an attic. The dormer window had shutters. I found they were screwed tightly closed. Unfortunately, I was in evening clothes and therefore I did not have my usual concealed set of tools. It is strange that in adversity how one picks on some trifle to divert the mind from the circumstances in which you find yourself. What I did was to use the shaft of dawn sunlight coming through a crack in the shutters and the hour hand of my watch to determine the direction of north.'

'I've never heard of that, Mr Holmes' said the superintendent.

'Simple, you point the hour hand to the sun and halve the angle between it and the twelve o'clock number on the dial of the watch. I determined that the house was aligned approximately north west to south east. If we now assume the house would have been aligned at right angles to the river bank that enables us to narrow down a stretch of the river which flows south west to north east.'

We studied an ordnance survey map. Holmes said, 'I am inclined to place great importance on the fact I heard one of those in the boat questioning whether there would be enough water because the tide was nearly out. Now, if we look at this note on the map it indicates the point near Richmond where the tide ceases to flow so we need not concern ourselves with any place further upstream.'

'The Thames Division officers will be able to tell us more about that,' said Shershay. 'I propose we retrace your journey. If you agree, we will take a police launch and travel upstream as far as Richmond. You recall that you were on the river for about an hour which suggests we limit our search to the stretch between Brentford and Richmond.'

'A splendid idea, Superintendent. May I also propose that once I am on board the launch you cover my eyes so that I can concentrate on sounds?'

We went aboard a police launch. Once we had passed Chelsea Reach and its church with the distinctive chime, Holmes' eyes were covered. As we progressed up stream and passed under a bridge, he said, 'I recall the distinctive sounds as we went under the bridges.' Further on he said, 'I believe that's a railway girder bridge.' A few seconds later he provided an important clue. 'We are going under a stone built bridge. I do recall that the two bridges were close together.' One of the river policemen holding the map put his finger on where the railway bridge and the road bridge at Putney were close together. As we progressed further upstream there came the distinctive and not unpleasant smell of a brewery. 'Ah, yes, I certainly recall the aroma of a brewery,' said Holmes.

'That's the Stag brewery at Mortlake,' responded Shershay.

After we had passed under Hammersmith Bridge the launch slowed and we scanned the dwellings which lined the bank along the stretch of the river that flowed south west to north east. None of them was substantial enough to match Holmes' recollection of being held in a large mansion. Furthermore we were convinced that the most important thing was the reference by the villains to the state of the tide.

The river police had been asked to arrange our journey so that when we reached Richmond the tide would either be right out or nearly so. Once past Brentford, more and more of the muddy foreshore was exposed. By the time we came alongside the grounds of Syon Palace, moorings and boat houses were standing on mud rather than in water.

'What can you hear, Mr Holmes?'

'There is a lot of noise over to my right. I remember that when we stopped. I also remember there were hardly any sounds to my left. Where are we?'

'We are approaching Isleworth village,' said Shershay. 'At this point the river runs south west to north east. Kew Gardens are on our left and that is why you heard few sounds. We are just passing a large house facing the river on the boundary of Syon Palace. That may be the one we are looking for.'

'We may as well let you see,' said Mycroft.

Holmes uncovered his eyes, blinked a few times in the light and then looked at the large mansion. As there was still some daylight, the launch was not stopped because we did not want the occupants of the house to be aware they were being scrutinised. We went a short way upstream and stopped for a discussion on what to do next.

'Mr Holmes, that large mansion has a boathouse. Could it match your recollection of where you were prisoner?' said Shershay.

'Yes, the boathouse and the dormer window on the river side face south east which suggests it is more than likely the house we are looking for. Its position on the boundary between the grounds of Syon Palace and Isleworth village is significant. Particularly, as the map indicates, there are no other houses alongside the river between here and Brentford. Can we turn and go past it again? When we do we should make ourselves less conspicuous. If the villains are in that house we want them to see only the usual crew.'

With some difficulty the launch was turned without becoming stuck in the mud. Once more we went past the house.

'Look,' exclaimed Holmes, 'there is the window. You can see the shutters are still closed. It faces the right direction. And, I can also see the stone steps leading from the boat house. I distinctly remember stumbling up them.'

'Then, you are now certain, Sherlock, we have located the house?' asked Mycroft.

'Yes, that must be the one.'

We went back downstream as far as Brentford where we visited the police station and asked the inspector of the local force to provide an escort. By this time it was mid evening, and cabs were hired to convey us and some constables to Isleworth village. There we left the cabs and approached the house on foot as silently as possible. The only sound we made was the argument taking place between Shershay and the inspector from Brentford. The latter was uncertain as to what was intended. He considered that we had no right to enter the premises without the authority of a magistrate; particularly after dark. Whereas, Shershay argued that as he represented Scotland Yard and that a known criminal was likely to be in the house then we were justified in our actions. He said he would take full responsibility.

We gathered on the doorstep. Despite Shershay pounding on the door with his fist and shouting 'Open in the Queen's name,' there was no response from within. 'There's nothing for it.' Selecting the largest of the constables he said, 'I see you have large boots, my man. Force the door.' The door succumbed to the strength of the law, or rather its boots, and we rushed in. We could only see as far ahead as the lamps held by the constables. However, we could make out that the house contained a hoard of valuables. Each room was the repository for a particular class of spoil: ceramics, including Ming vases, in one room; in another, silver plate and silverware; paintings in another and so on.

After we had lit some of the ornate oil lamps a search started for Tresscot-Jones and his confederates. We did not find anyone. Holmes decided that he would like to examine the contents of the study. He was anxious to know whether his thoughts on crime that had been extracted from his mind, had been set down in writing.

I went with Holmes into the study leaving Shershay and the others to make an inventory of the stolen goods. There were many bundles of papers and letters. Holmes had hardly started to go through them when he said, 'Watson, these are from those who Tresscot-Jones has been blackmailing. Many of these letters are from notable people including from minor members of the royal family. They were having to pay large sums to avoid their secrets and lapses of morals being exposed.'

'Blackmail is an evil trade which leaves its victims often powerless to resist its demands,' said I.

Suddenly there was slight noise and I was aware that someone had entered the room. There then followed the sound of the door being locked. We both turned and were confronted by none other than Tresscot-Jones. He must have been hiding and had emerged to confront us. He was pointing a revolver at us.

'Do not move. I can shoot you both before you could reach me Holmes.'

'Tresscot-Jones again,' said Holmes.

'Yes, and I am about to dispose of the country's foremost obstacle to my activities. I should have finished you off the other day when I had you in my power. A double dose of the drug and you would never have woken. As for you, Doctor Watson, you will now have to leave this world at the side of your companion.'

As Holmes had related earlier, Tresscott-Jones' voice was full of cold menace. So much so that my blood froze in my veins. Any thought of a desperate bid to seize his gun was dispelled by the fact that I was literally turned to stone. I could not move a muscle. All my senses were concentrated in my vision. As if through a magnifying glass, all I could see was his finger tensing on the trigger of his gun.

'Click'. For a split second there was silence. The gun had misfired. Before the cylinder could revolve just one step and move the next cartridge into position, Holmes leapt forward and knocked the gun out of the villain's hand.

What followed was a blur of flying fists, thrashing limbs and wrestling bodies. Just as I attempted to come to the aid of my friend, one of his fists inadvertently hit me and I went backward over the desk. Before I could regain my senses and rejoin the fray our antagonist had thrust the heavy desk at me. I found myself pinned between it and the wall. Fortunately, by the time I had pushed it away, Holmes skill with Oriental methods of combat had overcome the wiry muscles of the villain.

I examined my friend's battered head that had been assailed by the villain's weighted stick, and was relieved to find no serious damage; although one side of his face would soon be black and blue. At that moment the door was forced by the local constabulary and Scotland Yard's finest, who had been drawn by the noise of commotion. Holmes briefly explained what had occurred.

'Mr Holmes, we'll take Tresscot-Jones back to Scotland Yard for questioning,' announced Shershay. 'Do you say the letters you found show him also to be a blackmailer?'

'That is so, even a cursory glance through them revealed the names of some most important people who were having to hand over vast sums to avoid being exposed over some embarrassing detail in their lives. He has obviously tried to take the place of that other evil monster Milverton. You will recall he met his death at the hands of one of his victims. I suggest, Shershay, all the letters must be burned. If any were to get into the hands of Fleet Street our escape from death would be wasted.'

On our return to Baker Street I immediately sat down to write a rough account of all that had happened since Holmes had set out to a violin concert. As I did so he said, 'I presume you have in mind writing a sensational tale. If you do so, please do not attribute to me unbelievable skill and strength in overcoming that villain. It was a close run thing, my dear friend. Had his gun not misfired you would now have the task of writing my obituary in which, I anticipate, you would also exaggerate my prowess.'

THE END

THE DARK ON DARK MYSTERY

Part One: The Illusionist

In which a visit to a theatre demonstrates to Sherlock Holmes and Watson how a cunning thief was able to steal both a secret appliance developed for the Royal Navy and a valuable painting

We were on our way to the royal dockyard at Chatham; travelling down by train from Victoria station on the London, Chatham and Dover railway. Once again I was accompanying my friend as he started on another case. This time it involved the theft of a recently developed device that would be essential for the ability of Her Majesty's ships to fight. As little of the passing scene could be observed because of the fog, I used the opportunity to read the many personal notices inserted in the newspaper by those who offered quick cures for many different ailments, some seeking a response from a missing relative and others arranging a rendezvous.

Holmes had instilled in me the knowledge that many of these small notices, perhaps no more than three lines, could be the foundations of intriguing stories of frustrated affections and the seeds of criminal activity. Indeed, I had in recent times become addicted to reading the terse messages. As we progressed I became aware that my companion no longer seemed to take any interest in my comments on particular items in the paper or in the passing fog-wreathed countryside. His replies were brief. He seemed not to hear what I was saying. Frequently he glanced at his watch or the timetable.

'At last!' he exclaimed as the train began to slow down at a station. Before it had even come to a standstill he opened the door, leapt out and began to stride briskly along the platform and disappeared from my view. A few minutes later the guard blew his whistle, the driver responded on the engine whistle and the train began to move. At the last moment Holmes leapt into the compartment and slammed the door behind him. I could see that he was much relieved.

I assumed there had to be two explanations, at least, for his brief absence. One, during the journey he had been composing in his mind a telegram to those who would be waiting for us at our destination and he had gone to the telegraph office. Or, two, a matter which propriety prevents me dwelling upon. As we progressed Holmes began to question me about some railway matters.

'Are any of the trains on this line formed of vehicles having what I understand is called a corridor whereby we can walk the length of a carriage or even pass onto an adjacent carriage? I remember I travelled in such carriages when I was in America. At the end of each car, as they term their carriages, there was a small convenient room for the obvious comfort of the passengers on journeys taking many hours. I also observed that an American train was not only far more commodious than ours but the carriages were all of the same size. On this line in particular a passenger train has the appearance of the castellations of a Norman fortress because the carriages are of different heights.'

I responded. 'Corridor trains are being introduced on some of the railways for their principal express trains. However, the Chatham has yet to acquire them. Although they seem to offer what the traveller desires, there are many who oppose the idea of internal communication. I have read about those of a nervous disposition, and females travelling alone, who are fearful of being robbed or assaulted by someone gaining access to them from the corridor.'

'I can understand such concern, Watson. However, I would welcome such a facility and if I were a betting man I would wager on their use spreading over the next few years.'

'Unfortunately,' I replied, 'the railway companies may not wish to upset their shareholders by what, to them, may seem an extravagant arrangement and not really necessary. The line on which we are now travelling is notorious for its parsimonious attitude to passenger comfort. This carriage was built over thirty years ago.'

The discussion on passenger comfort subsided into a few monosyllabic replies and ended. However, my mind continued to be occupied with the possibility of villainy in a carriage having a passageway along its length. I began to mentally construct a tale involving a detective, such as my great friend, having to solve a crime, a murder for example, whilst the train continued to rush through the night. The detective would be in the same situation as that of the crew and passengers in a vessel many days from land.

Then the flash of inspiration came to me. 'Why don't I write such a tale?' But then I hesitated. Holmes would vent his scorn on such a proposal. Therefore I would have to use a nom-de-plume. I recalled that one of my nieces had the ambition to emulate the Brontes, Mrs Gaskell and Jane Austin, but she wished to write not about society and social habits, but about the detection of criminals. As she explained, few girls had attempted such a subject. I also realised that if I were to write such a tale then I would not be inhibited by the need, as when recounting Holmes' cases, to avoid sensation, drama and exaggeration. I should be able, when necessary, not to let the facts spoil an otherwise interesting plot.

As we progressed toward Chatham I continued to mull over the idea of becoming a writer of tales of mystery and adventure. But then thought why should I? I had enough writing to do, keeping up with Holmes' activities and recording them.

When we arrived at the dockyard at Chatham we were met by Admiral Collingwood and another officer. The admiral was a commanding figure. Although he was dressed in a black frock coat and waistcoat and grey trousers and not a uniform, his full beard and bushy eyebrows along with a piercing gaze left one in no doubt that he preferred the quarterdeck to being in command of a shore establishment. I noticed that he turned his head to one side when we spoke which suggested to me that, along with his loud voice, he was somewhat deaf.

The two officers emphasised their concern over the loss of a 'device'. They also explained why they had decided not to call for the help of the dockyard police or the official police. 'The fewer privy to the circumstance the better,' said the admiral.

When Holmes inquired about the nature of the device we were told that it was so secret that only the inventor and a few senior officers understood its function and its purpose. Holmes response was, 'Admiral, you wish that I should determine how the loss occurred, yet you cannot tell me anything about the missing thing or object. Is it as small as a snuff box or as large as an elephant?'

'All I can tell you, Mr Holmes, is that it is about the size of a shoe box.'

'Thank you, Admiral, for that information. I hope it will assist my investigation. Now may we inspect the scene of the robbery? That is, I presume a robbery, and not just a case of it being mislaid?'

'Undoubtedly robbery, as I will explain,' was the reply.

We walked over to a long low building which I learned was a ropewalk. Another storey had been added at one end, which was entered by a covered external staircase. The admiral explained that the inventor of the missing device had the use of the upper end of the building as a workshop. There he had experimented with, developed, and built a small machine whose purpose was essential to the future of the Royal Navy. The device was always kept in the workshop. It was never taken to any other place.

Before we went up the enclosed exterior staircase Holmes spent a few minutes surveying the outside of the building before asking, 'Admiral, is that staircase the only way up to the workshop?'

'That is the only one, Mr Holmes. As you can see the windows are barred even though they are out of reach from the ground. We have taken great care not only to keep the device secure, but also have endeavoured to ensure that its presence is a secret even within the walls of the dockyard. Mr Halden Carpet, its inventor, is waiting for us in his workshop.'

At the top of the staircase there was a small landing with an alcove in which were a number of cleaning implements, such as mops and brooms. The door to the workshop had a substantial padlock. In response to a knock, it was opened. Facing us was an elderly man with a shock of white hair. His posture indicated that he was afflicted with arthritis and his spectacle lenses were of a type for alleviating short sightedness.

'Afternoon, Carpet,' shouted the admiral.

'Name's Carbet with a b, not Carpet,' was the inventor's response.

'Quite so, quite so. May I introduce Mr Sherlock Holmes and Dr Watson? They are here to investigate the loss of the device.'

The inventor ushered us into a long workshop whose equipment and contents were in a confusing jumble. I was reminded of the state of our sitting room after one of Holmes' 'experimental' days. He showed us where the missing object was usually kept when he was not working on it. Holmes inspected each of the windows, benches and cupboards. I observed that he spent some time looking up at the rafters which were exposed. In a few places planks had been placed across the beams in order to provide more storage space.

After Holmes had put questions to the inventor relating to the most probable time when the device was found to be missing, we left. Before leaving the dockyard Holmes stood away from the ropewalk and gazed at the roof from both sides.

'Have you seen something of interest?' I asked.

'I need to consider whether someone has removed any of the tiles and gained entry to the workshop that way. However, I cannot see any have been disturbed.'

As we travelled back to Baker Street I refrained from interrupting Holmes' thoughts; I was certain he was going over in his mind what he had heard and seen at the dockyard. I occupied the time by considering the lives of the thousands of people who lived in the houses that bordered the railway. Most of the dwellings were of modest size and placed close together. I surmised that each held secrets; some interesting, some tragic and even some in which a crime had or was about to take place. When the train went over the junctions at Herne Hill he spoke for the first time. 'Watson, may I see the sketch plan I asked you to make of the workshop?'

His only comment, after studying my attempt to make a faithful representation of the plan of the workshop, was, 'possibly, yes, it might be.'

The next morning Holmes was reading one of the newspapers; dividing his attention between the words and his toast and marmalade. 'It seems that the spate of jewel robberies from houses in Belgravia continues. I am surprised that Superintendent Shershay, who is mentioned here, has not sought my, I mean our, cooperation.' He paused. 'Mrs Hudson has certainly provided a most excellent marmalade,' he said.

'Well it could be that Shershay is too proud to ask. After all he has been dependent on your skill for some time now and must want to succeed on his own.'

'Could be, Watson. Yet I never attempt to take sole credit for solving a crime. It is most important to avoid upsetting the official police. In the majority of cases their presence is essential to ensure the legality of our actions.'

'Yes, I agree. By the by, do the reports in the papers of the jewel robberies, which have attracted your attention, indicate any common feature?'

'Well the most significant is the absence in nearly all cases of any signs of forcible entry. The windows and doors have not been forced. Furthermore, the absence of soot in any of the hearths has eliminated the use of small boys being sent down chimneys.'

Nothing more was said for a few minutes during which we applied our thoughts to different possible methods of gaining entry to a property without leaving any trace.

Then I had an idea and said, 'When we were in the dockyard you examined the roof of the ropewalk building to see if any of the tiles had been disturbed. Could such a way into a building be the one used by the Belgravia villain?'

'Indeed my dear fellow that could be the method of entry. I wonder if Superintendent Shershay has considered it. My knowledge of the limitations of the Criminal Investigation Department at Scotland Yard suggests there may not have been a careful enough inspection of the roofs.'

'Then, should he not be advised to examine them more closely?'

'I suppose I must, but he will not take kindly to such advice.'

One evening later in the week we went to the theatre. We sat in a box close to the wings of the stage watching performances of magic. We shared an interest in demonstrations of slight of hand and the appearance and disappearance of objects seemingly without human intervention. But, of course, we were well aware that hidden human hands were somewhere on the stage. It so happens on this occasion we were able to discern a figure clothed entirely in black who was assisting a magician.

The 'all-black' assistant moved heads, limbs and objects around the stage.

'There's the reason why the police have failed to see the Belgravia robber,' whispered Holmes.

On our way back to Baker Street we discussed the possibility of a criminal who dressed from head to toe in black to conceal all but his eyes. Furthermore we decided he was likely to be extremely agile. 'Someone able to move from roof to roof, cross voids and, possibly, enter through attic windows,' said Holmes.

'I agree with you. Such a cunning villain could move undetected across roofs and gain entry. However, how could he then move down through an occupied house to a lower floor where jewels he sought might be kept? Surely most households in Belgravia remain alert throughout the night?'

'Some, Watson, I am sure, will keep a special guard on their valuables but I regret to say many would be satisfied that the exterior of their property was so thoroughly secured at night that they had nothing to fear.'

The next morning I ventured, with some trepidation, to interrupt Holmes' enjoyment of his breakfast. 'Have you had any further thoughts about the man in black and the Belgravia robberies?' I asked.

'I confess I had little sleep last night because my mind was on the Chatham case rather than robberies in Belgravia.'

'Did you come to any conclusion?'

'If you do not mind, old chap, I would rather keep it to myself for the moment. We will now have to make another visit to Chatham. Do try some of this marmalade. It is so good that I might say it is addictive!'

I did not respond because I had become accustomed to Holmes preferring to keep a conclusion to himself until he was absolutely certain that it was the correct one of a number of possibilities; as well as to his habit of suddenly changing the subject.

And so one hour and thirty five miles from Victoria station we again arrived at Chatham. At the inventor's workshop Holmes made another close study of the contents and position of the door, windows and other fixed objects. At one point he persuaded the inventor to leave the door open and then, sotto voce, he asked me to move quietly, from where the device had rested on a bench, to the door, and to go out onto the landing at the top of the external staircase.

As Holmes occupied the inventor with questions, so that his back was to me, I moved round the open door and out onto the landing. Then Holmes asked the inventor to show him exactly the steps and actions he took whenever he had to leave the workshop.

'Now, Mr Carbet,' said Holmes, 'I see that you unlock and open the door and then you go to the lever that operates the two electric lamps. You turn the lamp off and then you leave, locking the door from outside. I noted that there are two electrified lamps hanging from the rafters. Why do you only have one illuminated?'

'The dockyard dynamos cannot produce enough electricity for all the lamps in the dockyard to be lit at the same time.'

'I see. So, when you leave this part of the workshop, in which you keep the device, it is in darkness.'

'That is so.'

'Now Mr Carbet I have an important question to put to you. A few moments ago while you were showing me the drawings of one of your inventions were you aware that Dr Watson had gone out onto the landing. You obviously did not see him but did you hear him?'

'Well, no.'

'I thought not,' replied Holmes. 'I have to tell you that whoever stole the device had been hiding here since you first entered after returning, as you told me, from having tea with one of the dockyard officers.'

'Surely that cannot be. There was no one with me when I came back and unlocked the door.'

'I am certain there was someone. He was dressed all in black, was small and lithe and more than likely had been concealed behind the mops and brooms on the landing awaiting your return. As you opened the door he was right behind you. When you turned in the dark to feel for the lighting lever he slipped silently past you and possibly swung himself up into the rafters to await an opportunity to steal the device. Unfortunately your impairment of hearing was to the advantage of the villain.'

'Do you mean to tell me, Mr Holmes, that when I left that evening he could have been moving behind me and carrying the device?'

'Just so.'

'Where is he now and where is my device?'

'All I can say, Mr Carbet, is that we have to find the villain before we can find it. Find him and that, I hope, will lead to the missing device. This case is far from over and you may not hear from me again for sometime. Good Night.'

Following the conclusion concerning how the thief had been able to steal the device Holmes appeared to have lost interest in the case. It was a few days later that our breakfast was interrupted, not for the first time, by Superintendent Shershay.

'Good morning, gentlemen.'

'Welcome Superintendent. No doubt you come on official police business,' responded Holmes. 'I see in this morning's paper that the residence of the Earl of Clonkelly was the object of the most recent burglary in Belgravia.'

'The Yard seeks your help, Mr Holmes, in determining how a most valuable painting was stolen. Unfortunately I have to confess that we cannot make any progress. The villain or villains appear to have been able to enter the earl's house without being frustrated by some especially secure doors and windows. The thief took only the one item.'

'Just a painting, you say?'

'Just so, Mr Holmes. Perhaps you and Dr Watson might have the time to come with me to the scene of the crime. I am sure there might be something of importance that my officers have failed to see.'

'Agreed, the sooner we can get there the better because time tends to wipe away important evidence. Can you come Watson?'

'Of course,' I replied.

Shershay explained that the family had gone to their Irish estate for the hunting season and only a few of the servants had remained behind. So we were free to inspect all parts of the house. The missing painting was *The Coronation of the Virgin* by Fra Angelico.

'I am most surprised by what you say. Surely, the famous painting hangs in the Uffizi gallery in Florence?' I asked. 'I had read recently that Edward Burne-Jones, one of the so-called Pre-Raphaelites, was so inspired by it that he renounced his intention to enter the church in favour of becoming an artist.'

'You could be right, Dr Watson,' replied Shershay. 'The reason why the earl does not want its disappearance reported in the papers is because it is the subject of a dispute over which is the genuine Fra Angelico. The one in Florence, or the one which we have to find. A telegram received from his lordship in Ireland, in reply to mine, requested that the matter be kept out of the papers and, should any one inquire, we were to say that only a number of jewels had been taken.'

Holmes started his investigation by studying the front of the house and then we walked round the end of the terrace in order to reach the mews at the back. The mews was a busy scene: the dense fog of the past few days had gone and lines of sheets and linen were drying, horses were being groomed and carriages polished.

Shershay lead us through the servants' door where we were met by the housekeeper who first showed us the set of rooms used by her and the butler. Further on, through a labyrinth of passage ways, we reached the servants' hall.

'I observe that there are two sets of stairs leading up to the ground floor,' commented Holmes.

'That's right,' replied the housekeeper. 'These only go as far as the hallway and the main staircase, but the back stairs connect these quarters with each floor of the house.'

The housekeeper confirmed Shershay's observation that none of the windows, or either of the only two exterior doors, had been forced or showed any signs of an attempt having been made to open them.

'Let us now look at the room in which the painting was hung,' said Holmes.

At the back of the principal reception room on the ground floor was a curtained alcove from which the painting had been taken. As we examined the empty frame I ventured to comment 'these curtains will have allowed the thief to cut and remove the canvas without being seen.'

'I was thinking the same, Doctor,' said Shershay.

As we were examining the alcove I noticed Holmes stoop down and pick something up. He said nothing and I did not comment. There then followed a minute inspection of the hallway and the stairs leading down to the servants' quarters.

At the bottom of the stairs there were a number coal scuttles lined up against a door. 'I presume this door is for the coal cellar? Is it bolted at night?' Holmes asked.

'Well no, there's no way into the house through there,' replied the housekeeper.

'Except, I presume, there is an opening in the pavement to allow the coalmen to deliver the coal.'

'Of course, Mr Holmes. It's the usual type; only a small hole and its closed by a heavy iron lid.'

As we were leaving Shershay asked, 'Mr Holmes, have you come to any conclusions as to how the burglar managed to get in and how he was able to leave carrying the painting?'

'At this moment I have few ideas. I will need time in which to consider a number of particular and singular aspects of the crime. However, before we leave I must examine the window on each of the landings of the servants' stairs. As we have observed, all the windows of the basement and the ground floor are fitted with bars.'

On our return to Baker Street Holmes became absorbed in some chemical experiments. I did not interrupt him because replies to any questions would be in the form of mumbled grunts. As with all his diverse activities Holmes applied his mind to them with the utmost determination to solve a problem. He did not welcome being disturbed. He would so concentrate his mind on a problem that any questions or comments put to him fell on deaf ears, or, occasionally, prompted a grunt of acknowledgement. However, I confess I was much tempted to ask if he had had any further thoughts about the robbery at the house we had just visited. But I restrained my impatience.

It was not until after we had had afternoon tea when Holmes returned to the subject of the stolen painting.

'Watson, I have been reviewing the recent robberies in Belgravia and in particular the removal of the Fra Angelico. The first and singular aspect is, with the exception of the last robbery, the thief or thieves took all they could get their hands on.'

'To my mind there is one fact common to all the robberies,' I opined. 'This was the ability of the criminal to move in and out of the premises without having to force doors and windows. You demonstrated at Chatham the manner in which the robber had been able to enter and leave the workshop without the inventor being aware of his presence. However, the latter's deafness and short sightedness were to the advantage of the thief. Whereas, in the Belgravia house there were servants whose sight and hearing were not impaired. Furthermore, are you of the opinion then that the spate of burglaries in Belgravia and the theft of the painting are not necessarily the work of one and the same thief or gang?'

'Just so. I am inclined to believe that the last robbery was the work of someone who was not responsible for the others. The fact he took only one important item and left others of equal or greater value, in monetary terms, suggests he knew precisely what he was after. Whereas, with the other burglaries the thieves took anything they could get their hands on. Furthermore such a conjecture leads to the possibility he was acting on behalf of one of the more important members of the criminal fraternity.'

'Have you someone in mind?'

'Well not yet. However, I am convinced the thief was also he who stole the device from Chatham. You have just commented Watson, on how I determined the way in which he had entered and left the workshop without being seen, and had concealed himself in an extremely small space.'

'Therefore you think there is a common factor in the theft of the Chatham device and the painting, even though they are significantly different items to be of interest to the thief?'

'Indeed. They are different and tonight we are going to stand outside the stage door of the magic show theatre.'

Once again, my friend switched his mind from one thing to another virtually in mid sentence.

'I cannot see what good could come of such a strange activity. Those who do so usually carry a bunch of flowers to bestow on one of the lady performers whose charms cannot be resisted.'

'Of course, Watson, we must arm ourselves with flowers otherwise our loitering might attract undue attention.'

Later that evening we stood among the cluster of admirers outside the stage door. Eventually the performers started to leave. 'Now, Watson, keep an eye out for a small man. About the size of the one dressed all in black who assists the illusionist.'

We waited in vain. No small man appeared. In reply to our question the doorkeeper said, 'all the ladies have gone. Looks as if you've bought some flowers for nothing. Try another night gentlemen.'

Not wanting to draw too much attention to our presence we left. The next evening Holmes decided we should disguise ourselves as loafers and stand on the other side of the alleyway leading to the stage door. I was dressed in one of the many types of different clothing that Holmes kept for the purpose of being able to disguise himself.

'Watson, observe that hansom out in the street. It was there last night in the same place, and one of the female performers joined the man in the cab who was waiting for her.'

'Nothing strange in that. Could be her husband or her lover.' I replied

'Possibly, but all the same we need to attend a performance again. I have reached a conclusion which you may find unbelievable. However, for the time being, I shall not burden you with it.'

At the first opportunity Holmes obtained tickets for the front row of the stalls. 'The first violin would do better playing a banjo,' he whispered. Other sotto voce comments on the quality of the orchestral strings followed.

'Now with this act, Watson, watch closely how the girl is made to disappear.'

The illusionist invited members of the audience to inspect the floor of the stage and observe that a section bounded by posts and ropes had no trapdoors. Holmes was quick to take the opportunity of examining the boards.

The act commenced with a woman standing in front of the illusionist and within the area of the stage which had been inspected. In front of her was a girl. Although the stage was not well lit I could see what was happening. The woman swung the girl round so that she was between her and the illusionist. That is what the audience was intended to see. But when the woman stepped to one side the girl was no longer there.

After the performance I persuaded Holmes to take supper at Simpsons; one of his favourite restaurants in the Strand. With coffee Holmes, in deference to other diners, smoked a cigar rather than his pipe. Over brandy I raised the question of how the girl was made to disappear in full view of the audience.

'I suppose it was the usual use of mirrors. Am I right?'

'Not this time. I noted that the woman who swung the girl round had voluminous skirts. The girl went under them and somehow was carried off the stage.'

'I should have seen that.'

'Not necessarily. Nearly everyone in the audience was no more observant than you.'

'A clever trick indeed,' I said. 'But has it anything to do with the Chatham and Belgravia affairs, and is that why you have taken such an interest in the performances of illusionists we saw at the theatre?'

'Precisely, my dear fellow. And I am now going to put to you what may seem an astonishing conclusion.'

'Which is?'

'The Chatham theft and the robbery of the painting were the work of a girl. I will go further and conclude that it was the girl we saw tonight on the stage being made to vanish.'

'Why did I not think of such a possibility?'

'Habit. We do not usually associate the fair sex with major robberies. Among petty criminal activities I suppose there are as many females as men involved. Of course, poisoning and stabbing are just as likely to be the weapon of a woman as that of a man.'

'Therefore, you are of the opinion that the painting was stolen by the girl we saw at the theatre? If I recall correctly she was billed as Miss Lilly Longtree.'

'I am certain of it. You may recall I was able to speak to two of the constables whose beats passed the earl's house on the night of the robbery. One of them remembered he had passed a man and a woman embracing close to the house. He had assumed they were lovers and that one or both were servants. He also mentioned, and this is important, that the fog was so thick he suddenly came upon them.'

'I assume that one of them was the girl Lilly Longtree?'

'Yes, that it what I have decided. Now my reconstruction of how she made her way into the house depends for its veracity on her ability to get though the coal hole. If she was able to then she would have gained the coal cellar. From there she went up the stairs to the hallway and from there into the reception room.'

'I must say Holmes you seem to have provided an acceptable explanation. Except that lifting the heavy cover of the coal hole, surely, would have been seen by someone not least by the constable?'

'Not if the woman being embraced by the man was a mannequin. The girl provided the leg movement as the couple approached the house. Once in position over the coal hole the girl bent down within the mannequin's skirts and with the help of the man, lifted the lid of the coalhole. She then slipped down into the cellar and closed the cover behind her. The man then supported the mannequin with his arm round 'her' waist and went away.'

'Yes, I follow your sequence of events and realise that the female thief was then able to move through the house and cut the painting from its frame. But, surely, Holmes, she could not have gone back through the coalhole unless the man was waiting for her. How could he be certain about how long she would have been in the house? She must have had to wait for an opportunity to reach the reception room without being seen and then she had to get back to the coal cellar. As the housekeeper told us, the servants took it in turn to stay awake and watch the ground floor rooms.'

'I admit that was something which exercised my mind for some time until I recalled that, when we were examining the doors and windows, I noticed that the catch on the back stairs landing window of the first floor could be moved without difficulty. Had Shershay's men been more observant when they first examined the scene of the crime, they may have seen that the window catch was open. I have concluded that the thief, carrying the rolled-up painting, went up to the first floor, through the landing window, closing it behind her, down the adjacent drain pipe and away. She could not get through any of the ground floor windows because, as we saw, they were all barred.'

'I can picture this clever girl dressed overall in a tight fitting black costume moving silently through the house, sliding under furniture and hiding motionless behind curtains and furniture. I suppose we have reached the end of the case. All Shershay has to do is arrest Lilly Longtree and recover the Chatham device and the painting. I suppose we also have to consider who employed her as a thief? I cannot accept that she acted on her own accord.'

'Just so, Watson As you say, she was unlikely to have acted alone. Whoever put her up to the burglaries could be among the dozen or so master criminals that I have listed. Had not Tresscot-Jones been eliminated I would have placed him top of the list. As the girl was commissioned to steal two entirely different objects then it must mean her criminal master has more than one client. One mystery is why steal a painting whose provenance is doubted? As for the theft from the naval dockyard I would expect that one of the clients is an agent of a foreign power. Both may require further investigation. I will report my findings and conclusions to Shershey as soon as we return home.'

'Oh, I forgot to ask you about the object you picked up from the floor of the alcove?'

'It was a dull black button from, I had concluded, a black suit or, as we now know, an overall black costume. That was an excellent supper Watson. Time we repaired to Baker Street.'

Part Two: The Cobra

It was only after Holmes had successfully solved the mystery of the Vanishing Chambermaid that he turned his attention again to the Chatham and Belgravia cases.

I came down to breakfast one morning to find, not to my surprise, that my companion had spent the night curled up in his old chair rather than in bed. The atmosphere in the room was redolent with the effects of the many pipe fulls of tobacco that had been smoked. I did not stand on ceremony but went immediately to one of the windows and opened it wide. I anticipated he might protest, but was determined to have my way. To my surprise he did not protest despite the fact that he was never one to enjoy fresh air for the sake of its benefits. He said nothing. Perhaps he realised that even for him the atmosphere might be likened to that of the Inner Circle of the underground railway during its busiest times.

'Did you sleep well, old chap?'

I replied, 'tolerably well, thank you. I presume you have been up all night wrestling with some problem.'

'Yes, I decided that the missing naval device and the painting require my attention. I have had a number of thoughts on the subject. I have discarded most of them. One of those remaining is that the house in which that very clever young girl lives has to be searched very thoroughly. As Shershay informed me the other day, she continues to refuse to say anything. He has tried everything, other than physical abuse, to make her talk.'

'Surely,' I responded, 'Shershay's men must have searched there.'

'Oh, indeed they have. But, as you know, my dear fellow, the official police when making a search are handicapped because they rarely have any idea of what they are looking for. They also do not apply a scientific or rather, I should say, a methodical approach to the task.'

'I presume you will spend some time in the house at first doing nothing but contemplating the environment before, as one might say, "opening drawers and cupboards and looking under the mattresses".'

'Every day, Watson, you absorb more of my methods of detection and deduction.'

Accompanied by Superintendent Shershay, we went to the girl's rooms in the upper part of a villa that had once been, as an estate agent would have described, a desirable property in a desirable neighbourhood, Now the road had fallen from a desirable state to an indifferent one, and the house with it. Holmes indicated how the superintendent and I should conduct a methodical search and the objects that needed particular attention. For his part he repaired to the girl's bedroom and sat on the bed. He neither said nor did anything. I knew that he was absorbing the atmosphere and the contents of the room. He was also imagining the time that the girl had returned and, mentally, he followed all her movements.

After thirty minutes Holmes showed us a stick of black greasepaint. An obvious clue considering the method she had used to move around unseen. He also found hidden between two sheets of drawer-lining paper, that the previous search had missed, a plan of the ropewalk and its loft at Chatham. A significant feature on the plan was the annotation in German.

I drew attention to the framed photographic portrait of a man whose age suggested it was her father or a close relative. 'Is this important?' I asked.

Holmes replied, 'It could be, I am contemplating it. I need to take it back with me so that it can be studied under a better magnifying glass than the one I have with me. There is a possible clue that may reveal that the gentleman is a member of an organisation whose existence I would have discounted. I would have assumed that that organisation had been wound up or dispersed after the Royal Academy Affair of 89. We must consider some of the items in the girl's wardrobe. Look at this dress. See, the quality and the expensive decoration and finish? We must also consider this mirror and the other items of beauty equipment. Their mountings are all hall-marked silver. Furthermore, this small jewel box contains a large sapphire of, I expect, great value. The question is, why does she have them?'

Later that day, with the aid of a powerful magnifying glass, Holmes began to study the photograph we had taken from the girl's house. 'Now look at this, Watson. If you study the man's right wrist that has been exposed, because the sleeve of his shirt has moved up when he adopted a Napoleonic stance, you should be able to make out a strange tattoo.'

'Yes, it is a pair of entwined snakes. Is that significant?'

'It is very significant, Watson. It is the badge of the one-time Snakes criminal fraternity. They may no longer be one-time. They may have come to life again.'

'As this photograph may have been made some time ago I do not see that it provides a positive indication, Holmes, that the Snakes have been reformed, revived or become an active part of the criminal world again. I am going to remove it from the frame and look on the back.'

'As any skilled detective would do.'

I removed the photograph and examined the back. 'Ah, the photographer has obligingly marked the date. It is ten years ago. But, surely, this is not a positive indication that he is still either alive, or if he is, is a member of a criminal gang?'

'My dear fellow you are right in that assumption. However, as I have to confess, I am grasping for straws when it comes to finding clues. Reluctantly I need to make an assumption, and that is that the person in the photograph is a relative of the girl. More than likely he is her father, and furthermore he may be directing the criminal activities of his daughter.'

For a day or two the Chatham and Belgravia cases were dormant. It was only when Holmes was making his customary study of the small notices printed in the Times and the Telegraph that they were revived.

'Listen to this, Watson. "Two reptiles seek those who sleep." There's a post restant address.'

'Reptiles, you say. Of course the gang that you think has become active again. If you are right then all Shershay has to do is watch the post office named and arrest who ever arrives to collect the letter.'

'My dear chap, it may not be as simple as that. I doubt very much that a member of the Snakes would collect a letter themselves. No, they would pay some minnow of the criminal world to collect it for them. All the same I will advise Shershay to put one of his men to watch and follow who ever collects any letters.'

It was not long before we heard from the superintendent. Apparently a youth had collected the letters from the post office and had been followed. He did not go far before he handed them over to a minor member of the local criminal world. He was followed until he was lost among the dark alleyways of Limehouse.

'Well the search has been narrowed,' said Holmes. 'Once again I shall have to disguise myself and go down to that horrible part of the capital and see if I can find where the Snakes gather.'

'Shall I come with you? You could be exposing yourself to danger.'

'No, old chap, thank you, but I am confident that my disguise will be one that will provide a reasonable degree of protection.'

Holmes did not return until well after midnight. In the morning he told me what had happened.

'The first thing I must tell you, Watson, is how very effective my disguise was. I can laugh now at what happened but at the time I may have been in some danger. You see, I was walking back towards the City hoping that I might find a cab when I was accosted by a well dressed gentleman who made advances.'

'Advances, advances, what do you mean, old chap?'

'My disguise was so effective that he assumed I was one of the ladies of the night. He became very aggressive when I resisted his advances and he attempted to floor me with his walking stick. He was very strong but eventually my straight lefts and upper cuts persuaded him to leave.'

'What an interesting encounter. I am glad you have come to no harm. Did you find the Snakes' lair; if that is the correct term for a gathering of reptiles? I suppose 'snake pit' is more appropriate.'

'More appropriate than you might believe because they were down in the cellar of one of the houses close to the river. I found out where they were by following a villain whose face I recalled from a previous encounter. I even had the temerity to accost him. As I attempted to interest him in going with me he kept on walking and eventually he disappeared into one of the derelict houses that abound in that part of the docks. I was then able to work my way round the back of the house and could see, through a small window that looked down into the cellar, the gathering of the Snakes in their pit.'

'Could you recognise any of them?' I asked.

'Apart from the one I had accosted, none of them was a familiar face. I was disappointed at not seeing the man in the photograph, although I did manage to just hear scraps of the conversations that indicated there was a leader they called 'Cobra'.

'But the Cobra was not there.'

'I gathered that there would be another meeting in two days time at which the leader would join them. What I must do is let

Shershay know what I have discovered and suggest he should be prepared to arrest the Cobra and his gang.'

After a meeting with the Superintendent, Holmes and I agreed to accompany him and some of his officers to Whitechapel and watch the premises in which the Snakes gathered. It was another of those occasions which I call 'a Lestrade night'. In other words, a vigil in the cold and rain.

After three hours Shershay decided to send his men in and arrest the Snakes hoping that the Cobra would be among them. Back at the local police station we were disappointed to find that none of those arrested was the Cobra. They were all well known habitual minor criminals. We returned at three in the morning to Baker Street where Mrs Hudson had left a cold supper for us in the sitting room.

After refreshing ourselves we sat smoking and discussing the night's events. I was in the chair to the left of the fireplace and facing the windows across which had been drawn the heavy velvet curtains. Was it my imagination? Did one of the curtains move? A draught perhaps? But both doors were shut and the fire had been banked up for the night. I thought nothing more of it and decided to finish my cigarette and retire. My eyes were very tired and I may have dozed off for the next thing I recall is a growling voice. 'Do not make a move or I'll have to shoot you both.'

There, standing by the table was a strange creature. Short or rather, as I recalled later, squat. Broad shoulders, long arms and very short legs. Perhaps not more than four and a half feet tall. His brow jutted out over the deep-set, coal-black eyes. In each hand was a revolver of a calibre out of keeping with its owner's size. One pointed at me, the other at Holmes.

Holmes for some reason did not appear to be surprised at our visitor's sudden arrival. 'The Cobra, I presume.' Holmes' comment was delivered in a calm but ice-laden voice.

I saw that the facial structure was, indeed, similar to that of a cobra. The hooded brow lent a menacing aspect.

'I anticipate that you must have learned I was investigating your criminal activities and now you are about to stop it.'

'Mr Holmes you are right. But before I complete my task I need to find out what you know about the Snakes and what you have told Scotland Yard. Of course, you are now going to say that under no circumstances will you answer me. I anticipated such and therefore I am going to shoot your companion unless you tell me what I need to know.'

As the hammer of each gun was cocked the threat was real.

'Well, well, Mr Cobra, or what ever your real name is. I am in no position to refuse. My companion's life is far more valuable than the dossier I have compiled on the activities of your gang. May I reach for it? It is just here on the shelf.'

The Cobra waved one of his pistols to indicate that Holmes could reach for the dossier. Not that it was any consolation, but Holmes had picked up one of his commonplace books. He half rose from his chair and proffered it with outstretched hand. As he did so he let it fall.

'Clumsy of me,' he said as with one sudden movement he pulled the edge of the rug on which the Cobra was standing. Both guns fired. One bullet actually passed through the hair of my head. The other struck the slipper in which Holmes kept tobacco and lodged in the fireplace surround.

Holmes displayed the hidden tiger in him. He was on the villain in a flash. A few vicious blows with the edge of each hand crippled the Cobra. Even though he was barely conscious, we took no chances with him. By the time Mrs Hudson arrived, having been woken by the gunfire, he was trussed up to one of the chairs.

'I'm not going to interrupt what little is left of the night and summon Shershay,' said Holmes. 'Mrs Hudson please arrange for a telegram to be sent to Scotland Yard as soon as it is a convenient time in the morning. Just say the Cobra is at breakfast with Sherlock Holmes.'

In the morning Shershay came to collect the Cobra. He was surprised at what he saw. 'He's not on our wanted list. I do not understand how we've managed to miss him. Cunning fellow indeed.

Later, as I was writing an account of the case I realised that there was a question relating to the identity of the man in the photograph in the girl's room which we had assumed was her father. When I mentioned it Holmes said, 'Watson, assumptions can be the start of many a false trail. It is of her father but he died some years ago without his membership of the Snakes ever being discovered. He was not the leader of the gang as I had assumed.'

'Holmes, another question which has arisen and one on which I would have expected you to comment on before now, is how did the Cobra get into our sitting room undetected by Mrs Hudson?'

'The reason I have not mentioned it is because I have to confess I am completely baffled. I need a few more pipe fulls and undisturbed contemplation of the puzzle before I can provide you with an answer.'

The next day Holmes said, 'Watson, I cannot believe my own stupidity. I've been solving the mystery of the girl in black and, as you will recall, we both considered that access to a premises might be gained through the roof. Here I have been resident in 221B for some years without ever bothering to entertain the possibility of a burglar, for example, gaining entrance unobserved through the skylight of the attic.'

'I too have never contemplated such a happening,' I responded.

Standing looking up at the hatchway leading to the attic Holmes said, 'Watson, please ask Mrs Hudson if you can borrow one of her brooms.'

Holmes raised the handle end of the broom until it touched the hinge end of the hatch. He then pushed upward and the hatch lifted up.

'The cunning Cobra must have come through the skylight and unscrewed the hinges of the hatch from above, so that he could then lift the hatch and pull it away from its bolt. I am certain that a close examination of the bolt will find marks on it that confirm my deduction. Mrs Hudson will have to summon that chap who does odd tasks to see that the skylight has not been damaged and is secure.'

The Cobra was persuaded to admit his crimes and the painting and the secret device were recovered. Holmes received a generous reward for his detective skills and   passed a generous portion to me.

THE END

THE WRECKER

*In which Sherlock Holmes determines the identity of the
wrecker of trains.*

For once breakfast at 221B Baker Street was not interrupted by
a telegram requesting my friend's help in solving a mystery or
tracking down a murderer. After he had done justice to bacon
and eggs followed by curried chicken and then generous
helpings of marmalade on his toast Holmes proceeded to
enhance, or rather pollute, the atmosphere with the smoke from
one of his old pipes. I could see that behind those half closed
eyelids his mind was going over some unsolved case.

A bold headline in the newspaper I had just opened caught my
attention and I could not restrain myself from breaking into his
thoughts. 'Oh, what a dreadful disaster,' I exclaimed.

'What has happened?'

'There has been a smash on the Central British that has killed
over a dozen and injured many more. This is the second major
disaster suffered by the railway this month.'

'I presume the author of the item in the paper has included as
much gory detail as he can and I expect added some
embellishments of his own.'

'Yes he has, and as usual the paper pontificates on the cause of
the accident and demands that such an event must never occur
again. My grasp of railway matters may be rudimentary but

when reading the report of what was supposed to have happened it is clear that its author is completely out of his depth when describing the way in which a train moves, how it can be stopped and how the signals and points work.'

'Ah, I recall, my dear chap, your apoplectic outburst when you read last year in a paper how its reporter had questioned why a driver of a train had not steered out of the way of an obstruction on the line, as if he was at the helm of a ship. Among the ill–informed opinions expressed in the newspapers concerning the accident, is there one that you would consider acceptable?'

'There is. The recollection of the eye witnesses standing on the platform at Milltown Junction, where the train was wrecked. They saw someone push a loaded platform trolley onto the line in front of the oncoming train. The heavy metal and wood frame and the steel wheels and axles of the trolley were too much for the locomotive's wheels to push aside. The engine was derailed, and slid on its side through the length of the station before turning across the tracks to provide a barrier against which the carriages were turned into a heap of splintered wood.'

'And the villain, I should say, murderer was not caught?'

'He was not caught. It seems there were a number of trolleys piled high with bags and parcels at the end of the platform that provided a screen for his fiendish act.'

'Fiendish, indeed, Watson.'

'The report also mentions the wreck of the Scots Express last month on the same railway. The cause of that accident was quickly determined by Colonel Rich, Her Majesty's Inspector of Railways. Apparently, the signal wires had been tampered with. The driver believed that his train would be directed along the main line as expected, and not, as it transpired, diverted at a junction onto an alternative route. At full speed the engine and tender overturned at the points leading off the main line and nearly all the carriages finished up in a tangled mass behind them.'

'A cunning and devilish act, I must say. The driver then had no warning?'

'None. Had the distant signal been showing a red light then the driver would have immediately reduced speed ready to stop at the junction signals, or pass onto the alternative route at a safe speed. Whoever the culprit was must have understood how the signals are worked. He was able to pull on the wire from the signal box so as to move the arm of the signal to the clear, 'off' position, and so display a white light.'

'The circumstances you have described offer an acceptable and simple explanation of the cause of the disaster.'

'However, Holmes, that would have required great strength as there is a counter weight at the signal to ensure that in the event of the wire breaking the signal would return to the 'on' position and display a red light at night. The appropriate lever in the signal box provides the necessary effort.'

Later that morning a letter came for Holmes by the second delivery. When he had finished reading it he passed it over to me saying, 'I do find coincidences come too readily in our daily lives. You have just been reading about railway accidents when, as you see, this letter has come from the Central British Railway.'

I read the request for Holmes' help in tracking down the one who had demanded large sums from the Central British Railway, and who had threatened that if they were not paid their trains would be wrecked.

The next day we were visited by two directors of the railway. They explained the circumstances and brought with them two letters from the perpetrator of the ghastly deeds. Both demanded payment of £10,000 and warned that failure to comply would result in further disasters on their railway.

One of the first and obvious questions that Holmes raised concerned whether the police had been informed about the letters. The answer was that they had not because to do so would reveal to the world the threat to the safety of the company's trains. It had to be recognised that there were newspaper reporters who, for a consideration, obtained confidential information from the police. It was well known that at some police stations there was an 'understanding', to the benefit of some senior officers, whereby newspapers became privy to matters concerning investigations and pending trials. On the other hand some would say that a close relationship between the police and the Fourth Estate was for the common good.

After we had discussed details of the case the directors left, leaving the letters for Holmes to study.

'This is the first time I have come across ransom or demand letters made up from pieces of handwriting,' said Holmes.

'The usual method employed is to cut individual words out of a newspaper or other printed material. Why choose this method?' I asked.

'I can only assume, Watson, that it was intended to confuse any attempt to trace the originator. Often when demands are made up of cuttings from newspapers I have been able to determine which newspaper, and from that find a clue leading to a criminal.'

'When the directors of the railway were here I sensed your reluctance to take on the case.'

'Indeed. This case is not the type I would usually consider because the circumstances involve matters which I find difficult to understand. Had it involved chemistry, biology, firearms and the behaviour of individuals and the ephemera associated with them, then I would be eager to apply my particular brand of scientific investigation. With this type of case there may be no discarded cigarettes, cigars and their bands, pipes and spent matches. With this case, I do not have to look for a cause. In this instance all I have to do is find either the motive or the villain.'

'I agree, Holmes, this is a wide-ranging case. There is no one place, such as a room, in which all the clues are concentrated.'

It was not until we were having supper that Holmes came back to the subject of the demand letters. 'The most significant thing about the handwriting, apart from the fact that the words have been cut from the writing of different persons, is that they exhibit the hands of both male and female, and there are spelling errors. Together they indicate that they were written by school children. Most have used a precise copperplate hand. I have also observed that on some of the pieces of paper pencil lines have been used to ensure consistency in their writing. All this leads me to the conclusion that the composer of the letters used pupils' exercise books which had been discarded.'

'Are you suggesting we are looking for a school teacher?'

'Only if there is a schoolteacher who has acquired detailed knowledge on the subject of railways. For the time being we have to assume we are looking for a railwayman because only he would understand the mechanisms of the railway.'

A telegram from the directors of the railway company suggested that Holmes might wish to visit the places where the trains had been deliberately wrecked. At first he was reluctant to do so because he could see no purpose in such visits. Colonel Rich, of the railways inspectorate had already issued his reports on both disasters; the causes of which had been quickly discovered.

When I asked Holmes how he was going to respond to the proposal of the directors he replied, 'I will visit the sites even though they cannot expect me to find any clues that could lead to the identity of the villain after all this time. He could have tampered with the signal wires anywhere between the signal and the signal box. As for clues on the platform, from which he pushed the trolley, I doubt there will be any. There are many feet that have gone that way since. I am only going so as to show the railway company that I am doing something to earn my fee.

We arrived at the office of Hector Wilsheer, the head of the railway's own police force and, after a short wait, we effected our introductions. Although he had not been expecting us we spent a little time in his office discussing the incidents and Holmes then asked to be shown where the wrecks had occurred.

Our first visit was to the signal box where the signalman had operated his apparatus correctly but to no avail because the villain had somehow managed to heave on the signal wire and move the arm to the 'off' position and so show a white light. Mr Hector Wilsheer was one of those men whose girth nearly matched his height. He might be described a solid block of a man, of which the head, arms and legs were just incidental appendages. He provided us with a summary of the strength and duties of the railway police.

I commented, 'I am right, am I not, in believing that in the early years of the railway, the constables' duties embraced operating the flags and lanterns that provided protection for the movement of the trains. And those duties were in addition to preventing trespass and the discouragement of drivers stopping their trains close to a public house in order to quench their thirst?'

Wilsheer nodded his head to indicate agreement. Throughout the time he was with us he rarely spoke. His replies were not often vocal, and at times his conversation was limited to mumblings and gruntings. I particularly found interesting the slang he used to describe the type of people he had arrested over the years. Apparently, on the railways there were those called 'drag-sneaks' that stole from luggage. Also there were 'snoozers', who would take a room for a night at one of the railway hotels, with the object of leaving the next morning with linen, towels, cutlery and any thing of value that could go into the especially large inner pockets of their greatcoat.

When we left the signal box we were then taken to the station, where the villain had pushed a loaded platform trolley onto the line just as an express was about to pass through at full speed. Although the debris had been cleared from the tracks and the platform, we could see some of the carriages that had not been completely destroyed had been moved to a siding. I was horrified by the terrible wounds they had suffered: sides torn away to expose the partitions and seats; roofs torn completely off; and ends stove in to the length of one or two compartments. I found myself thinking that the next time I boarded a train I would deliberately choose a compartment in the middle of a carriage and definitely not in the first or second carriage from the engine. Although, in having this thought, I observed from the state of the wrecked carriages that in a major smash each carriage became the destroyer of its neighbour. I decided I should have to trust to luck. Wilsheer was called away and we spent a few moments speaking to railway staff on the platform.

During our return journey by train we sat in a first class compartment that happened to be in the last carriage. Each time the train stopped I was no longer listening to what Holmes was saying. My mind and my ears were acutely tuned to the possibility of a train approaching us from behind. At one station I did hear a train approaching. Its progress toward us became louder and louder. There was a sustained shrill engine whistle. Was that a warning that Holmes and I were to meet a dreadful end? With a roar, a shriek, and a drumming of wheels an express passed our train on the adjacent line.

Holmes appeared not to have noticed my discomfort and continued to comment on the case.

On our return to Baker Street Holmes continued, 'Watson, we need to investigate the origin of the scraps of paper. Visiting the railway has served little purpose; although, no doubt, you found the environs of the railway most interesting.'

'I did. I also came to realise the destructive forces involved in an accident. Those wrecked carriages emphasised how little protection wood and glass affords a passenger. I have read that it is proposed to introduce metal carriages that will be more resistant to damage in an accident. However, with so many ideas aimed at the safety of passengers the railway companies, or rather their shareholders, see little profit in them. Trains would be heavier, locomotives would have to be more powerful and a company's annual coal bill would be much higher. Only recently have the railways been forced by legislation to equip their trains with effective automatic brakes and passenger communication systems, as well as better signals and points. As with the wreck at the junction, the driver of a train at night relies very much on his detailed knowledge of the track and the position of the signals so that he does not confuse the red light of a stop signal with that of a distant signal.'

'My, my, dear fellow, you certainly have immersed yourself once again in the minutiae of the railways. However, for the present let us concentrate not on signals, lights and matters mechanical, but on a human being.'

'Of course, you are right. I presume the threatening letters are still the most important clue.'

'For the time being they are. Perhaps the only one.'

'Holmes, I observed that when we visited Wilsheer's office you made a discrete scrutiny of its contents. Was that deliberate?'

'The answer is neither yes nor no. As you know I try to observe as much as I can of my surroundings. It was only when I saw that there was a pot of paste and a pair of scissors on his desk that an idea came to me which encouraged me to make a most detailed study of the room, whilst we spoke to him. I never discount anything or anyone during an investigation.'

'Ah, of course, the threatening letters were made up from individual scraps from handwritten documents. Do you feel that points the finger at Wilsheer?'

'Indeed it does. However the paste and the scissors are no more than circumstantial evidence. I say that because I also observed he had a number of typewritten slips pasted on the standing orders to the constables, which were to be placed on notice boards. However, on our arrival, as we waited for the door to be opened, I noticed a small piece of paper lying on the ground. Here it is.'

I read the handwritten words YOU MUST. 'Of course, of course, Holmes, it could be from another letter which is being prepared. We seem to have our man,' I exclaimed.

'I am not sure of that. We would still have to provide conclusive evidence of his criminal acts. Although Wilsheer has become a suspect, the evidence against him is rather frail.'

'But, surely, the letters are sufficient evidence of his crime?

'Possibly, Watson, but anyone could have taken discarded paper from a school and cut it up to make the letters. The pot of paste on the desk and the scrap of paper I found outside Wilsheer's door could be evidence of his complicity. However, such evidence would be figuratively torn to shreds by a lawyer. So far, this case proves to be far too simple and therefore enjoins great caution. One way of testing the validity of the evidence against Wilsheer is to consider the possibility that someone else wrecked the trains. In doing so we either find such a person or having eliminated them as a suspect we strengthen the case against Wilsheer. By the way, do you recall the photograph on the wall behind Wilsheer's desk?'

'Yes, a railwayman in his uniform.'

'It was a photograph of his father. I discovered, from careful questions I was able to put to a group of engine drivers that Wilsheer considered the company had treated his father most unfairly after he had been injured in an accident. They did not even offer him a place as a porter. Apparently the injuries to his father resulted in increasing lameness and pain and Wilsheer sought ways of easing his father's suffering. When I heard about that I recalled that in his office there was a letter, in German. Although I could only see the heading, I could see that it was from a health spa. It could be that the money demanded from the company was for treatment of his father at a spa in Germany. I doubt that he intended anyone should see it.'

'So there's the motive.'

'Possibly.'.

The following morning over breakfast I raised the subject of Wilsheer again

'You know you are always reminding me, Holmes, of the importance of the difference between seeing and observing. Well, I made an effort to do so when we were with Wilsheer. Of course, I had not the faintest suspicion that he could be the wrecker.'

'Excellent, old chap. What did you observe?'

'I could not help but note the precise geometrical arrangement of all the things on his desk and on the top of shelves and other horizontal surfaces.

'Splendid, keep on.'

'I am sure you recall that when you laid your hat and gloves on the small table by his office door Wilsheer immediately moved them so that your hat and gloves were juxtapositioned differently from the way in which you had put them down. Mine were also rearranged. Furthermore when you moved the square glass ashtray on his desk his hand shot out and re-positioned it so that it was geometrically at right angles to the edge of the desk.'

'Indeed, Watson, you have been observant. Now did you or have you reached any conclusions concerning Wilsheer's habits?'

'I have. Wilsheer has a significant obsession and one that I doubt he is aware of. His actions when moving things around are mechanical.'

'But, my dear fellow does all this have any relevance to our suspicions concerning him?'

'Only the possibility that those who have a marked obsession, particularly for ordered, pleasing, regimented patterns, can view any disorder in the world about them as something that has to be corrected. Possibly, I emphasise possibly, the injury to his father and his subsequent dismissal represented disorder.'

'A fascinating conclusion, although I cannot necessarily accept such reasoning. Perhaps you have absorbed too much of the

Vienna school of psychology. I find it difficult to accept the pronouncements of those foreign doctors who study the human mind and behaviour. However, in saying that, I do not want to disparage your attempt at observation.'

'Coming back to your idea of the possibility of someone other then Wilsheer, have you found one?'

'I have to admit, none.'

'By the way, I see that the share value of the CBR has fallen, presumably the result of the accidents.'

Holmes did not respond to my comment and I continued to cast an unprofessional eye across the financial pages of the morning papers. As I did so again the thought came to me that perhaps after all Wilsheer was not the Wrecker.

'So far, Holmes, we have considered him as the prime suspect because of what happened to his father. Could we be wrong?'

'I cannot answer for the time being. All that can be done is to investigate Wilsheer more thoroughly. So far I have yet to look into his family affairs. He is married and has children. What of his sisters, his aunts and his cousins?'

'However, if it is not Wilsheer, then could it be someone who was intent on affecting the company's financial standing and in some way profit from it?'

'An interesting thought, Watson. What little I know about the workings of the City could lead to such a conclusion. A telegram to Mycroft is needed.'

When Mycroft's reply came it suggested that the wrecker could be trying to affect the share value of the CBR with the intention of acquiring shares at a low price, in anticipation that in the future they would regain their former value.

I raised the possibility that it could be an official of the company. 'A possibility certainly but I doubt that it would be one of the directors,' was Holmes' reply. 'We are no longer in the 40s when some rather shady manipulations of shares took place. The share market is now more strictly regulated.'

During this discussion Holmes continued with another close examination of one of the letters. I watched him dissolve the paste that had been used to fix the pieces of paper in place. Once they had been dried and laid face down we could see that the original children's exercises had been written on the back of some printed material.

'Notice, Watson, the number of times the words 'inmates' and 'orphanage' occurs. They more than likely come from printed instructions relating to an orphanage. Perhaps you will allow me to test your powers of observation. Recall the visits we made to Milltown Junction station and Wilsheer's office at the end of one of the platforms. What did you observe?'

'An extremely busy station with many people milling about: some attempting to find seats in the two or three trains that were waiting; others bewildered by the problems of changing from one train to another; and porters pulling trolleys laden with luggage having to force their way along the platforms.'

'And the small child's terrified cries?'

'Why, yes, I do recall a mother assuring a child that there was no need to be afraid.'

'Afraid of what?'

'A dog of course. That amiable looking sheepdog.'

'My dear fellow surely you did not fail to notice the collection box strapped to its back.'

'Of course I saw it.'

'But, considering why we were at Milltown Junction, did you observe the name on the collection box?'

Suppressing my irritation at the critical manner in which Holmes questioned me, I answered, 'I am sure you did, Holmes'

'The Central British Railway's Orphanage, for the children of the company's employees. Thus we have the possibility that the letters were written on the backs of pages or notices concerning the running of the orphanage that happens to be not far from the station.'

Holmes perused one of the directories that listed all types of educational establishment, including orphanages.

'Listen to this Watson. The CBR orphanage includes on its staff a Miss Jane Wilsheer. Just another coincidence, that either is of no importance, or is significant. I trust that when you are writing up accounts of my cases you avoid when ever possible emphasising the role of coincidences. They should play no part in a scientific investigation. However, here we have a name, an orphanage, girls and boys being taught to write legibly and a supply of discarded paper on which to write.'

'That puts Wilsheer back on top of the list.'

'You know, Watson, another fact that came to me was Wilsheer's evasive answers to some of our questions about the accidents. He would change the subject or claim that he was a policeman not a signalman.'

'Yes, I did notice that, and also our unannounced visit to his office obviously confused him and his manner was most suspicious,' said I.

'Yes, of course. When I inquired about Wilsheer's career on the railway I learned that he started as a porter and subsequently was promoted to porter/signalman. Therefore, despite his avowed lack of knowledge about signals, he would have known how to pull the signal wire.'

Holmes was now determined to send a telegram to the company giving his opinion that Wilsheer was the criminal, and they should now contact the police. However, at that moment, through the window we heard the paper sellers crying out: 'Nuvver dreful smash on the railway.'

When I read the paper I was appalled to learn that another Central British train had come to grief. The question posed by the paper was whether it was just mechanical failure or was it yet another fiendish attack by the 'wrecker'? Apparently, a passenger train had run out of control down a long incline and been derailed on the curve at the bottom. The paper considered that the brakes must have failed.

Not surprisingly the two directors of the CBR were soon back in 221B Baker Street. They brought with them a scrap of paper on which were pasted the words PAY UP OR THERE'S GOING TO BE ANOTHER

The CBR directors reported that the cause of the disaster had been quickly determined. The shut off cock on the brake pipe at the back of the engine's tender was found to be closed. That meant that the driver had no means of reducing speed other than applying the hand brake on the tender and reversing his engine. By the time he realised what was happening it was too late. The speed had increased alarmingly. To interfere with the Westinghouse automatic air brake system the villain had had to reach across the gap between the tender and the first carriage and turn the cock just at the moment when the driver released the brakes and started the train. As it was night time no one saw him lurking alongside the train on the side away from the platform. The directors also said it required a specialised knowledge of how the brakes worked to be able to choose the right moment to shut off the brake pipe valve.

'Why did the guard not apply the brakes using the valve in his van?' I asked.

'He should have done so,' one of the directors replied. 'Apparently, he was writing up his journal and did not become aware of the excessive speed. He also mentioned that guards were reluctant to make even a small application of the brakes because a driver might resent such interference. By the time he realised how fast they were going he made a full brake application but it was then too late.'

Two mornings later Holmes related his conclusions to me. Miss Jane Wilsheer turned out to be the suspect's brother. She admitted that she had let him have discarded paper but had not asked why he wanted it. When no bank account was found for

Wilsheer and no connection with buying shares, Holmes decided that his motive was both revenge and concern for his father's well being. Had the money been handed over he would have had to keep it, as the saying goes, 'under his bed' until it was safe for him to transfer it to an establishment in Germany for the treatment of his father. Once Holmes had listed all the facts relating to Wilsheer's actions the police were informed.

No sooner had a telegram been dispatched to the railway when another arrived informing us that during the night Wilsheer had been run down by an engine. We learned later that there were two significant items found at the scene of the accident. One was a fishplate, a heavy slab of metal used to join rails together, and the other the tail of Wilsheer's coat that had been trapped when the points were moved over. It seemed he was intent on wrecking an express by jamming the points with the fishplate. He had not expected that the points would be moved to allow an engine to pass into a siding. Only at the last moment did the driver of the locomotive see a figure struggling to move away.

Holmes final observation indicated that once again his conclusions had been correct and it was the death of the villain in the act of trying to wreck another train which confirmed their validity.

'Justice has been done but in a most horrible way,' was my only comment,

THE END

NOTES

Until the signalling reforms of the final two decades of the 19th century a red light could mean either 'do not pass' or that the next signal was set at stop (red light) or indicate that the points it governed were set for a diverging route and therefore might require passing at a moderate speed. A green flag or light instructed a driver to bring his train forward prepared to stop; usually at the signal box. Eventually green was substituted for the white 'all clear' light but not until the second decade of the 20th century in Britain was yellow introduced in place of red as the standard indication of 'proceed with caution prepare to stop at the next signal'.

AN EAST WIND

In which Sherlock Holmes is able, with the help of research on the part of Dr Watson, to deduce how a body appeared on a railway embankment without footprints or disturbance of the surroundings.

As I have so often recorded, Sherlock Holmes' adventures and quests start with a telegram or a visitor during our breakfast. This particular morning was no exception. Holmes passed over to me a telegram which had just arrived. 'Read this, Watson.' He handed me the telegram. 'Once again The Yard is seeking my help.'

It came from Superintendent Shershay. I read how a body had been found in Kent and the local police were baffled. He would be pleased to know if my friend could travel down to a station on the Chatham line where he would be met.

'As I have little at present to occupy my mind, I shall accept Shershay's invitation. Perhaps you might come with me?' asked Holmes.

'Of course, I welcome a change from town life,' I replied.

For once I was able to persuade Holmes to travel on the underground railway. It was only a short walk to Baker Street station on the Inner Circle line of the Metropolitan Railway. From there we took a train to Farringdon Street and then another short walk and we were at the Chatham line's Holborn Viaduct station. Once our train had left behind the seemingly endless rows of the backs of the houses that crowded against the line, I began to appreciate the bucolic beauty of the Kentish countryside. I could not fail to question my decision to live in the particular environment and climate of London: the cold and dense fogs of winter; the stifling heat and unsavoury aromas of the streets in summer; and the sometimes unending cacophony from the street below the windows of 221B Baker Street.

We were met at a small country station by the superintendent. 'Good morning gentlemen. I'm pleased you were able to answer my request and that Dr Watson is with you. The local constabulary have called in the Yard because they are baffled and I must confess so am I. A body has been found half way up the side of a railway embankment and the cause of death appears to be uncertain. There are no visible signs of foul play.'

'Has the body been there for some time?' asked Holmes

'We cannot be certain. It was hidden from view because it was lying behind a bush and could not be seen by any one walking along the footpath at the bottom of the embankment. It is used by local people as a way through to the next village. Early yesterday morning the postman had his dog with him, as usual, and, like all dogs, it liked to investigate its surroundings. Its barking led him to the corpse.'

'Presumably the postman always passes at that time therefore we can safely assume his dog would have discovered it the day before had it been there. I doubt that mankind really appreciates and understands the skill possessed by dogs. I refer to their sensitive nostrils and the ability to detect and sort through the thousands of different scents that are around them. They could form, in addition to bloodhounds, a useful auxiliary force to the constabulary. I will have to examine the body. Did you find anything in the pockets of the deceased's clothing?'

'Just a sovereign, nothing else.'

'But in the meantime, Superintendent, I trust you took the precaution of avoiding unnecessary footprints around the place where the body lay.'

'I made sure of that. I remembered what you had told me about the need to avoid footprints and disturbing the surroundings when a body is found in suspicious circumstances. Therefore I instructed the local police not to move the body, even though it had already been there for some time, and it has been guarded day and night. Of course, there were footprints of the postman and later those of the local constable and my own.'

'Well, Shershay, let us hope that even those few do not prove to be too many.'

When we arrived at where the body had been found the postman and a constable were waiting for us. Holmes asked them and the superintendent to make an impression of the soles of their boots in a stretch of mud. Shershay then pointed out where the body was in the bushes half way up the railway embankment.

'As you can see, Mr Holmes, it would not have been easy for anyone to lift or drag the body up to there. To start with they would have had to lift it over the fence. Following your example in previous cases, I examined the grass and shrubs to see if there was any sign of them having been flattened or damaged in any way. I also looked for marks on the fence rails but found none.'

'I will go up and see what I can find.' Holmes climbed over the fence. We were about to follow when he said, 'no, please, everyone stay down here. The least disturbance to the soil and the vegetation the better.'

He spent some time contemplating the small space among the bushes. When he came down his expression was one of puzzlement. 'I have scrutinised with great care but I cannot think how the body got where it was and why.'

'Could the body have been thrown from a passing train?' I suggested.

'Yes, such a conclusion is a possibility, Watson. However, there are no indications, such as flattened bushes or grass, between the place where the body is and the top of the embankment, to support such a conclusion. Even though it is obviously the one anyone would draw when confronted with the facts as we know them.'

As we continued to discuss various possibilities a group of men working on the telegraph wires at the top of the embankment called out to us. 'What's happened?'

'Did any of you see any thing unusual yesterday morning? asked Shershay.

'Sorry, nuthin. We wer'nt 'ere then. Just come this morning to mend the wires,' was the response.

Once Holmes was satisfied with his examination of the area, Shershay ordered the body to be taken away. Later in the day he took us to the mortuary. As agreed, the clothing had not been removed. Holmes first inspected the victim's hands and nails, then noted the quality and amount of wear on the clothing; in particular he examined closely the cuffs and the bottom of the trouser legs. When Holmes started to search the victim's pockets he found, as Shershay had, they were empty of any thing which could have identified the victim. However, the labels were those of a well-known Savile Row tailor and therefore might provide positive identity of the victim.

'Shershay, you are certain no one has attempted to remove the clothing? Asked Holmes. 'Look, some of the buttons of the waistcoat have been torn off. Furthermore, it is deeply creased.'

'I gave strict instructions that the clothing remained undisturbed.'

'Of course. Now this is interesting. Look, these are not his clothes, they are too small. A most singular piece of evidence. Now, what about the boots?'

'Couldn't find them, Mr Holmes. We searched all-round but nothing.'

'So we have a body in clothes which are far too small and without any boots,' commented Holmes. He took out his large magnifying glass and examined closely the waistcoat.

He handed me the glass saying, 'Doctor, see if you can see what I see.'

At first I found nothing unusual but then I just managed to discern some small straw coloured fibres. 'Yes, I see what you mean. They might indicate that the victim had been bound by ropes.'

'My thoughts exactly.'

Out came another of the ubiquitous envelopes into which Holmes placed some of the fibres.

Back at 221B Baker Street Holmes busied himself with his different magnifying glasses and a microscope. I did not interrupt him. After a time he said, 'I will compare what I can see here with my collection of rope samples. I may be able to say with certainty from these fibres where the rope was made and what its intended use was. Now where did I put my magnet?'

The next morning as we were taking breakfast Holmes suddenly put down his piece of toast, heavily laden with marmalade, to exclaim, 'Watson I have come to a certain conclusion; one which may either prove to be nonsense or one that suggests how the body got to where it was found on the embankment.'

'Oh, that's interesting. You know, I spent much of the night pondering that question. I considered a number of possibilities such as the body had been conveyed along the path and then thrown to land half way up the slope. The intention being to hide it among the bushes. It would have taken a strong man to have heaved it over the fence. So I dismissed the idea.'

'Let us curtail our breakfast and get to Victoria or another Chatham line station as quickly as we can. We will take one of those ramshackle collections of carriages proceeding at a leisurely pace which the railway insists on calling an express.'

'Back to the scene of the crime then?'

'No, Watson, I doubt there is anything more of interest to be found there. I want to visit the village I had noticed lying a mile or two to the west.'

When we reached Victoria station we were just in time to catch the Down Dover Mail. Two hours later we were settled in a nook, along with bread, cheese and ale, in the principal inn of the village's two. Knowing Holmes' methods I refrained from unnecessary conversation because he put great store on what could be overheard in an inn.

'Did you hear anything of interest?' I asked as we waited outside the inn for the carriage we had ordered.

'The talk was much about the damage to the church parapet, the vicarage roof and to one of the chimneys of this inn. See, there is a pile of broken bricks.'

'Storm damage most likely,' I suggested, as Holmes prodded at the debris with his stick

'No, my dear fellow, something else, because I gathered from the conversations in the inn that, for the past three days, the wind in these parts has only been a breeze.'

'Shall we go and inspect the damage to the church?'

'That is not important. What is of singular interest is that standing here, and looking down the high street to the church and the vicarage, all three buildings damaged are roughly in a straight line. And, most peculiar is that length of bamboo lying with these broken bricks.'

'Of course, I see what you mean. If it was not the wind then it must have been some miscreant who climbed onto the roofs and set about causing damage. The fact that he proceeded in a straight line is, I suggest, a coincidence. Why did you remark on the piece of bamboo?'

'No particular reason.'

The answers to the questions we put to a number of the inhabitants indicated that none had seen anything during the night. Apart from those whose premises had been damaged, no one had heard anything unusual, such as a sudden fierce gust of wind during the night.

As we went back up to London I refrained from questioning Holmes about his interest in the damaged roofs because we were not alone in the compartment and because I anticipated he wanted to study undisturbed the other occupants and determine their occupation, state of health and even the reason for their journey. Of course, with all of the cases with which I have had the pleasure to be involved I had learned not to try and persuade him to reveal his most important conclusions; particularly after only a few days of investigation. I often sensed he had put his finger, as it were, on the most important item of the information gathered, thus leading to a successful ending, within the first hour or even minutes of inspecting the scene of a crime.

A typical morning in 221B Baker Street, such as the one I am describing, would find Holmes in his favourite chair surrounded by a cloud of tobacco smoke. Abandoned and scattered across the carpet would be the morning papers.'

'Much of interest?' I asked.

'If you mean, my dear fellow, of criminal activities which may require my attention then the answer is no. Apart, that is, of the body found by the railway line. Although, there is one story concerning a bank robbery which is in all the papers.'

'Where was that?'

'Tonbridge and before you enlighten me, yes I know it is on the South Eastern line to Dover.'

'Did they get away with much?'

'Indeed they did. £5,000 in five pound notes and, according to the reports, the robbers may have taken packets of newly minted sovereigns. As we often read, the police are baffled. The method of breaking into the bank and its safe, apparently, was obvious but who the robbers were, and to where they disappeared remains a mystery. None of the principal villains known for their interest in banks is suspect.'

'I am surprised the police have not requested your help. I am sure if you were to study the scene of the crime you could determine much about the robbers and even where to look for them.'

'Thank you for your flattering words. However, the body in North Kent is providing enough intellectual pursuit for the time being. Scotland Yard will, most likely, become involved when the county police run out of trails to follow. Then our friend Shershay will be called in and I will be urged by his superiors to help with that as well.'

Nothing more was said on the subject and Holmes re-applied himself to studying the fibres from the clothing of the body found by the railway line.

'Watson, this is interesting. These fibres are undoubtedly from the type of rope or hawser used in vessels and which could suggest that the victim may have had something to do with the sea.'

'Could they also suggest that the murder, if it is murder, took place in a ship or harbour and the perpetrator carried the body inland so as to confuse an investigation?'

'I agree there is such a possibility even though it is an unlikely one.'

The row of Strand Magazines on the bookshelf provided Mrs Hudson with another of her complaints about Holmes' habits. Nearly all had pieces of paper sticking up where he had marked a particular item of interest. I had to agree with her that it was most unsightly. On this occasion, on looking across the room from my chair, I saw that one of the issues was lying on the table open at a particular story. I did not get up to examine it as I assumed it concerned ships and their ropes

'Well I never. This is interesting!' Holmes sudden exclamation interrupted my careful study of a book on tropical diseases. A subject for which I needed to be come as familiar with as my companion, if I intended to assist him when ever I could with solving a mystery. He was reading the *Times* and, I presumed, must have come across a rare split infinitive.

'Something of importance?'

'Yes another attempt to build a flying machine able to progress without being at the mercy of the wind.'

'Is this anything to do with the mysterious body in Kent?'

'Indirectly yes. I'm fairly certain, as with the Sycamore Seed case, the body was more than likely dropped from out of the sky. The simple conclusion in this case is that it had come from a balloon which had progressed at no great height and had damaged some roof tops. You may recall a few days ago I was looking for my magnet. The reason being that under the microscope I observed minute black metallic slivers mixed with the rope fibres I was examining. Those proved to be iron filings. If one mixes iron filings with acid you get hydrogen gas which adds to my conclusion concerning the use of a balloon. I conclude that the fabric of the balloon had been damaged and that the gas was escaping. The occupants, or possibly a lone occupant, may have been jettisoning anything which was loose in order to remain aloft. I also surmise that during the attempt to lighten the balloon he may have accidentally lost his hold and fallen overboard. The balloon then lifted just enough to soar over the railway line but still caught the telegraph wires.'

'Holmes, you have made a remarkable reconstruction of a series of possible events. However, if you recall our flight in a balloon we were in a deep wicker basket and therefore it was not easy to fall out of. Furthermore, can we be certain about the direction from which the balloon had come?'

'Indeed, you have introduced an important fact. I agree it would not be easy to fall out of a balloon basket. We also have to consider a case of foul play. There may have been two men in the basket and following an argument and a struggle one was hurled to his death.'

'I see what you mean.'

'As for the path taken by the balloon, I noted that the village is down in the valley so its chimney tops are about level with the top of the railway embankment. If it had come from the east and cut the telegraph wires and immediately the balloonist had then fallen overboard it would have soared up and not clipped the top of the inn and the church.'

'What was the wind direction?'

'A significant factor, Watson. I have ascertained from the Meteorological office in Victoria Street that on that night the wind was from the east. However, a balloon could not have sailed, if that's the right word, against an east wind. Yet the sequence of events I have described required the balloon to progress from west to east.'

'Recently I read of the experiments being conducted by Lanchester and they reminded me of Hiram Maxim's flying machine.'

'Yes, I recall you showed me the learned paper by Lanchester. So now you consider that a dirigible aerial craft and not a balloon was involved?'

'For the time being it is the only reasonable explanation of how, what ever it was, moved against the wind.'

I was enjoying this exchange of ideas.

'Holmes, if this was a steerable flying machine then, as I understand how they work, it would sustain itself in the atmosphere because of the forward movement of its sails.'

'I think you will find they are called aerofoils, not sails. This particular aerial vehicle may have been some sort of balloon after all.'

'You are confusing me. First you argue against the use of a balloon and then you venture to describe a flying machine having aerofoils, which, as with the experiments of Lanchester, remains aloft because of its movement. Once any forward movement ceases then it falls to the ground.'

'Indeed, you have summed up the essential requirement. However, there is another type of machine combining the attributes of both the balloon and the aerofoil sustained machine. I refer, of course, to a dirigible buoyant ship of the air having machinery of some kind for propelling it forward.'

'Of course, I had forgotten about them.'

'As I have read, a number of inventors have been trying to develop a balloon which can be steered and has the means for pushing itself through the air. I conclude that we are indeed dealing with a dirigible buoyant craft capable of being propelled through the air by means of some type of engine. A number of clever people both in this country and in France are trying to build small but powerful steam engines for use in the air. I believe that about five years ago in France, a Clement Ader motivated his flying machine with a steam engine. Also Hiram Maxim, you will recall, nearly achieved what is now termed 'heavier than air' flight with his machine whose driving propellers were spun by a steam engine. Mind you, my research into the progress being made with aerial vehicles indicates that an engine, working on the principle of, what I understand is called, internal combustion, may prove in the end to have advantages over steam power.'

'Well, Holmes, you certainly have immersed yourself in the subject. I might even comment on how it is unusual for you to take so much interest in things mechanical.'

'It is not difficult to imagine a time in the future when aerial locomotion will be as familiar to everyone as the railway and ships. And, then, my dear fellow, my particular investigatory skills may be of use because, undoubtedly, there will be villains who will use aerial craft to further their ends.'

'So, if I am not mistaken, you have already decided that the body was dropped or fell from a machine which could sustain itself in the air and progress, if need be, against the wind.'

'Quite so. Now as you have taken a great interest in the subject I would be obliged if you could help my investigation by considering the use of a steam engine in an aerial vehicle.'

'I regret that my span of knowledge and experience is confined mostly to the medical world. I have been ever willing to be invited to attend post mortems of victims of crime and to comment on the effects of medicines and drugs. However, at times, things mechanical and science in general are beyond my intellectual powers. Although I must admit I have gained some knowledge of railway matters. Knowledge that at times has been of help to you. Nevertheless, I fail to understand why you need to know about such things. Surely the method of propulsion, let alone the design of steam engines, is irrelevant to the investigation?'

'My reason for such an interest in such a mechanical matter is because if we can determine the type of engine, its abilities and its needs, such as fuel, then we become closer to its owner or builder. From there we can progress toward the place from which the aerial craft ascended carrying, possibly, two people; one of whom was killed. I am not asking you to prepare a dissertation on steam engine design for use in the air. All I ask is that you consider some basic facts and give me an opinion. They are nothing more than answers to the following questions: what type of steam engine would be suitable; what type of fuel is the best for heating water to produce steam; how much water and fuel would be consumed on a journey?'

For the first time in my life I had to consider matters far beyond my ken. Eventually I presented my opinions in the shape of some notes; half of which were crossed out.

'Good, you've certainly applied yourself to the task Watson. Let us see what you have set out. One: the lightest possible steam engine. Yes, most important. Two: extremely hot steam. Why is that?

'My interest in railways occasionally leads me to magazines and books on the subject and I read recently about a difference of opinion over the advantages and disadvantages of especially hot steam. I regret I could not fully understand what was meant other than the hotter the steam the more effort it provides to drive the pistons.'

'Yes, you have confirmed some of my conclusions. Now, and this is interesting, you say that because a sufficient quantity of water needed for a voyage represents a great weight, then less would be required if some is recovered from the spent steam from the engine.'

'That is correct. Just up the road from here is the Underground whose engines are required to limit the amount of smoke they emit. They do that by sending the used steam from the cylinders not up the chimney to eject the smoke, but into the water tanks where it condenses back to water.'

'Oh, yes, I understand. Mind you, when we travelled the other day on the Underground there was still a great deal of smoke about, despite what you tell me about the arrangements made to limit its emission.

Now what have you to say about the fuel? You remind me the equivalent amount of heat from a ton of coal can be obtained from burning a far smaller weight of either a gas or an inflammable liquid. Watson, your study has been most useful in providing facts that I have missed.'

Another day passed. I had assumed that the case of the body on the railway embankment had either been forgotten or put on one side by both Scotland Yard and Holmes. Apart from a telegraphed message to Shershay, setting out his conclusions, Holmes did not appear to occupy himself with the case. It was obviously going to be somewhat difficult to proceed. For my own benefit I summarised the problem. One, who was the victim? Two, from where did the aerial craft ascend? Three, can we assume there were only two persons on board and that, if so, when and why did one of them fall out or was pushed out? Four, if this was a case of murder was it premeditated? But, above all, the starting point for all the mystery remained a mystery.

Nothing further occurred with the case for some days until I happened to turn a page over in the *Illustrated London News* and read about the work of an inventor who had at one time described an aerial machine capable of being steered and making progress against the wind. The writer informed readers that nothing more had been heard from the inventor for over five years. In the opinion of a number of learned scientists the machine, which had been described earlier, would be capable of dirigible flight over a considerable distance. Apparently the inventor had cut himself off from society and failed to answer any correspondence that might encourage him to continue with his work on his aerial machine.

Holmes was working at what I describe as his 'chemistry laboratory' which once had been a fine dining room table. Its one-time mirror-like surface was now pitted and scarred. I ventured to interrupt his experiment concerning the steadfastness of certain chemical dyes.

'Holmes, I am reading in this magazine about a flying machine that is presumed to be somewhere in East Sussex. Could it be the same machine that we surmise may have passed over Kent and from which the body of the unknown man fell?'

He paused in the middle of some experiment and I could see he was weighing my words. After a while he said, 'Watson, you could be right. A splendid conclusion, my dear fellow. Now let us study a map of East Sussex and find the place mentioned in the piece.'

'It's called Lower Arlington, a small village not far from Lewes.'

'Then that is where we must go as soon as possible. Please apply yourself to Bradshaw and find the next train to Lewes. I presume it is on the Brighton line?'

'Yes, it is on the branch which goes to Eastbourne and Hastings off the main line. Although, I may find we have to go into Brighton and change trains.'

With its customary stately, or rather, leisurely progress a train of the Brighton rail company took us to Lewes. At the station we hired a cab to take us to Lower Arlington. After a number of inquiries of the locals we directed the cabman to take us toward an isolated collection of farm buildings among which was a large barn.

'Holmes, I cannot say that I have ever seen a barn as big as that before.'

'Big enough, Watson, to house a flying machine of the type you have been reading about?' He ordered the driver to stop. We stood by the cab surveying the buildings and discussing what we could see. The cab driver interjected a comment. 'They don't like people noseying about. I advises you gen'l'men not to get too close. There's some vicious hounds kept there. They'll go for your throat if you get too close.'

'Do you happen to know what is in that large barn?' inquired Holmes

'They say, Sir, that there's a strange machine which comes out at night and flies above your head. A lot of nonsense if you ask me.'

'For the present, Watson, I have seen enough. We must return to the village and seek a lodging for the night'

The cabman took us back and we obtained rooms in the village inn.

In the snug that evening we listened to the conversations from the other bars with the usual object of assimilating local habits and customs. Nothing much appeared to interest my friend until his attention was alerted by hearing what the innkeeper was saying to one of the customers. 'That's the second time this week you've paid with a fiver. Lucky on the horses I suppose!'

As we were retiring and the innkeeper was shutting the doors Holmes said to him, 'I am surprised someone should pay for their ale with a five pound note'

'Now you mention it, Sir, there have been quite a few in the past week. There's two of them that used to work at the manor farm who had fivers. I suppose the owner paid them off in fivers. I can't remember the last time I'd seen one.'

'So the farm is not used anymore?'

'Can't be sure about that. All I knows is it's common talk around here about strange goings on and carboys and peculiar things delivered to the manor from the station. There's talk about a machine, not a balloon mind you, that can fly in any direction through the air.'

'Have you seen it?'

'Oh, no. And nobody else either. Even if there is one I expect the owner of the farm is having trouble getting it to work.'

The next morning, as soon as the post office opened, Holmes sent a telegram to Superintendent Shershay suggesting he join us.

When the superintendent arrived in the afternoon Holmes said, 'I realise my deductions could be wrong but I am convinced, from the evidence, that there is a link between the bank robbery at Tonbridge, a farm near here, and the body found by the railway line.'

'I am always willing to trust your judgement Mr Holmes, even though at times your conclusions seem most strange. Shall we inspect the farm?'

'We understand it is guarded by some fierce hounds therefore we must enlist the help of the local constabulary.'

The problem of the hounds turned out to be just a rumour. There was nobody in the farm. The large barn contained machinery and an apparatus for producing gas. Of greater significance and of surprise was the absence of a roof. Obviously this was where the flying machine had been built and from where it had ascended into the sky. As it was no longer there we could deduce that, as we expected, it had flown, damaged some roofs, torn down some telegraph wires and then disappeared. Furthermore, we were then in no doubt it was the machine from which the body by the railway line had fallen or been pushed overboard. Along the centre of the barn was a line of sand bags. Obviously, these had been used as ballast and dropped off to permit the machine to ascend.

Holmes commented, 'I observe from the trail in the dust of the floor that one of the bags was dragged along as far as the door over there. The question that comes to mind is why was it dragged and not lifted. See, I can easily lift one of the sandbags.'

I commented, 'Holmes, I fail to understand the significance of your observation,'

'As I am not completely certain of my deduction for the time being, Watson, I shall not burden you with it.'

Attached to the barn was an office which contained substantial amounts of paperwork, letters and engineering drawings which Holmes took some time to study. During our inspection of the rest of the farm Holmes climbed one of the large trees bordering a small pasture close to the barn. When he came down he led us to a particular spot and announced, 'Superintendent, I suggest we dig here.'

'Dig, Mr Holmes? Why here and what do you expect to find?'

'I have in mind that the inventor of the machine has not been heard of for some time. He may have been killed and his body hidden somewhere around here.'

The constables who had been enlisted unearthed the remains of a body. Holmes started a careful examination of the clothing. 'A singular fact, gentlemen, these clothes are not his,' he said. 'They are far too large in size for this person and they have not been buttoned up. Furthermore, I find it most unlikely that a scientist, if that is who these remains are, should have absolutely nothing in any of the pockets; no notebook, pieces of paper, watch chain, keys or money. I conclude that the clothes on the unidentified body which fell from the flying machine were those of the scientist.'

'A most acceptable conclusion, Mr Holmes,' responded Shershay.

'Superintendent, I should like to take with me the drawings that were found in the scientist's office as well as the letters written in German. Do you agree?'

'Certainly, Mr Holmes. I am sure you can make better use of them than the Yard. Please let me have them back when you have finished with them because they are evidence.'

'Of course.'

Back at Baker Street Holmes summed up the case.

'We have two bodies. Each has met a dreadful end. The report of the post mortem examination of the remains at the farm reveals that the skull had been severely fractured. We might conclude that the other body fell accidentally from the flying machine or was pushed overboard, although I doubt there was a third person involved. As we can see from these plans of the machine, an openwork construction of bamboo provided accommodation for the propelling machinery and the aerial navigators. It provided a precarious perch for anyone attempting to flee with, I presume, the proceeds of the Tonbridge bank robbery.

In the absence of other indications I am inclined to the theory that there was indeed an argument between the two men. But this was on the ground and not in the air. The scientist, for a motive which will for ever remain a mystery, was party to the bank robbery. His companion decided to flee with the money and when frustrated by the scientist, killed him. He had gained sufficient knowledge concerning the control of the machine that he was able to ascend and fly away. But to where? The letters may provide the answer to that. As for the machine; well we can only conjecture that it continued its voyage until its supply of fuel was exhausted. Then it was at the mercy of the wind or to the moment when insufficient gas remained to keep it aloft. Perhaps a search of the marshes on the right bank of the Thames may come across its remains?'

'Holmes, how did you know where to dig to find the body of the missing scientist?'

'Fairly simple, Watson. By climbing up into a tree I could look down and observe if on any part of the meadow the flora appeared to have been disturbed.'

'We also have the question of the clothing on the first body. As they came from a well known tailor, surely, Holmes, they provide a definite identification?' I recall you emphasised the fact that some of the buttons had been torn off and the garments were creased.'

'I have to confess, Watson, I stretched credibility by assuming that the wearer had, for some reason or other, taken the clothes of another man. He had, in fact, as we discovered, forced himself into the clothes of the scientist. I conclude that he did that in order to give the impression that it was the scientist who had absconded in the aerial machine. What I find strange is that the scientist did not keep anything in his pockets. That is no longer important, but had he done so then the clothes on the body by the railway line would have provided some early clues'.

'Most interesting. Now, what about the sandbag you observed had been dragged across the floor of the barn?'

'I deduced that it had contained not sand but many sovereigns. Whoever was in command of the flying machine had felt that it would not be able to ascend even when the sand ballast had been dropped. He therefore decided that he had to sacrifice the gold coins. And those coins were from the bank in Tonbridge.'

'So where are the sovereigns?'

'I anticipate that Shershay's men will come across them if they make a thorough search of the farm.'

'But does that not suggest that the one who took the machine intended to return?'

'A good question, Watson, and if he took the trouble to hide the sovereigns at the farm that was possibly his intention. But I doubt it. I believe that once he had killed the scientist he realised he had to flee to another country and there start a new life with the £5 notes from the Tonbridge bank robbery. The answer may be in these letters. Now let us apply ourselves to translating from the German.'

'Not a task I look forward to, dear chap, German handwriting is often difficult to read, even more so when my understanding of that language is not that good.'

With the aid of a dictionary we managed to make out that the letters were from someone in Cuxhaven. The scientist had also kept copies of his replies, also in German, to each of the letters he had received.

'I am sure you will agree, Watson, this correspondence is all about someone or persons trying to persuade the inventor of the aerial machine to fly it to Germany. If he were to do so he would be rewarded handsomely. What may be of significance is the source of the letters. Cuxhaven is a German naval harbour. The author could be an agent of the imperial navy.'

'Undoubtedly, as the more recent letters indicate, the scientist had no intention of undertaking such a voyage. I am sure I was able to translate one of the letters accurately enough to show that the distance the machine could travel would not have been sufficient to reach across the German Ocean.'

'This means the motive for killing the scientist was not just to abscond with the stolen bank notes but to gain the large sum offered if the machine were delivered to a place near Cuxhaven. The villain was either unaware of the machine's limitations or chose to ignore them. Greed was his downfall.'

'Despite the scientist's reluctance to sell his invention to a foreign country, which was a noble decision, he must have been party to the bank robbery.'

'Of that I am certain, Watson. This could be a case of someone who was so dedicated to their work that they had no scruples when it came to where funds to continue his work came from. I would not be surprised to hear, when Mycroft has had an opportunity to consider the case and examine all the documents we have found, that the scientist had made a number of unsuccessful representations to our own naval and military authorities attempting to gain their interest.'

'Once again, we have been involved with a case of a head in the sands attitude on the part of those responsible for the safety of these islands.'

'Another thing, Holmes, which has exercised my mind is, why were there no boots on the first body?'

'I admit, dear fellow, it was something which provided me with a great deal of thought. That is until I recalled that when we examined the room in which the scientist designed his flying machine there was a pair of boots. Nothing, you might say, remarkable but when, as we now know, the murderer had taken the scientist's clothes he found he could not force the small boots on and therefore set off barefooted.'

'You know you asked me to investigate the relationship between the quantity of fuel and that of the water needing to be carried.'

'Your conclusions were most helpful, Watson.'

'Well, these papers suggest that the scientist had relied on an unusual and especially economical fuel. One that provided tremendous heat from a small quantity. It is referred to as Ostoff.'

'Ah, of course, the carboys delivered from the station. They may have contained that somewhat potent and lethal liquor which we encountered in the case you sensationalised as A Liquid Mystery.'

And so, once again, I had become party to one of my companion's investigations of a crime involving machines.

All around we were seeing more and more mechanical marvels, such as flying machines, each providing an opportunity for the unscrupulous to take advantage of their wonders to engage in criminal activity.

THE END

THE DEVIL'S TOOTH

In which Sherlock Holmes has to find a stolen horse and track down the leader of a gang of betting fraudsters. Both he and Watson are once again confronted by a familiar villain.

I was standing at the window looking out of the sitting room in 221B Baker Street endeavouring to emulate Sherlock Holmes' undoubted ability to determine much about those passing by below. In the minute or two during which someone was within sight he could tell me what their profession or trade was, the state of their health and their finances, and from whence they had come and to where they were going.

As I applied my mind to studying a rough character leaning against the nearest lamp post my mental exercise was interrupted by seeing a four-wheeler stopping immediately below me and from which emerged Superintendent Shershay of the Yard and a gentleman. I assumed we were about to be visited. I was not mistaken. A moment later they entered our sitting room. The man with the superintendent was impeccably dressed. However, his clothes gave me no indication of his profession and definitely none from which I could deduce why he needed to see my friend. One thing I did observe was a gold device formed from entwined initials hanging from his watch chain. Perhaps that was of significance.

Shershay greeted us. 'Good Morning, Mr Holmes and Dr Watson, this gentleman, Mr Cartwright, has suffered a great loss.'

'As Superintendent Shershay has brought you to me then I surmise that a valuable horse has been lost or stolen.'

'Sir, how could you know,' exclaimed his companion.

'It is my business to know such things,' replied Holmes.

'It is very valuable,' responded Cartwright. 'It is Son of Malvolio. It has been stolen. That is why I have asked Scotland Yard to help.'

'The scoundrels who took your horse are, presumably, those who place large wagers and who are not averse to violence to further their ends,' said Holmes.

'We have no idea know who they are. Mr Cartwright has received this letter that demands a large sum for the safe return of the horse,' said Shershay, handing it to Holmes.

'Presumably, the absence of the horse as the favourite affects the odds offered on the other horses and, in the convoluted ways of the betting world, the villains hope to gain,' observed my friend.

'Essentially, that is what this is all about,' replied the superintendent. 'The villains have already placed bets at long odds on two of the other horses entered for the Rockingham Stakes. If this gentleman's horse does not run then they stand to gain much.'

'Superintendent, it appears, not for the first time, I am being asked to look for a horse'

'Nothing more, nothing less, Mr Holmes,' was the reply. 'Except, of course, we also want to catch the villains who perpetrated the crime.'

'Mr Cartwright, do you think that who ever took your horse intends it harm,' said Holmes. 'I doubt that such a famous animal could be disposed of as if it were a jewel.'

'Yes, its distinguishing marks make it recognisable to anyone,' replied the owner. 'As for their intentions I can only guess.'

'We can all agree, I am certain,' said Holmes, 'that the horse has been kidnapped either to affect the outcome of the Rockingham or to demand the ransom for its safe return. Or, even both.'

'Either way, Mr Holmes, I will be glad to get him back.'

'Then I will be at your stables tomorrow as soon as the South Western railway can manage to cover the sixty or so miles from here. In the meantime, may I keep the letter, Superintendent?'

'Yes. I am certain you will be able to apply your scientific detection methods and determine who sent it.'

The next day we arrived at the Cartwright stables set in a hollow of the Wessex downs. It was a relief to be away from London. So far August had been very hot and with hardly any wind. The streets produced a pungent aroma and the air was full of dust.

We were taken to the place on the long gallop where the horse and its rider had been ambushed. Apparently, the latter, who was the head stable lad Jacob Waters, had been pulled off his saddle by two men wearing masks. He had struggled with them but received a blow to the side of his head that stunned him. His hands and legs were tied with ropes and he was left at the side of the gallop. He watched the two villains lead the horse through the gate that gave access to the bridle path that was close to the gallop. After they had gone he was able to untie the ropes and run back to the stables

Holmes studied the soft ground of the gallop but admitted he could not find any particular hoof or foot marks. At that point he stooped and picked up a small gold cravat pin in the shape of a horseshoe. After examining it closely he said, 'I presume there are many of these worn among racing men.'

'That is so, Mr Holmes,' replied Cartwright.

'Ah, what have we here,' Holmes was holding up a florin.

'Is that significant?' asked Shershay.

'Possibly. It could suggest that the thieves tossed the florin to decide between two courses of action. However, why they had to do that when this, obviously, was a carefully planned robbery, requires clarification. One explanation could be that there had been a last minute change of plan.'

From where we stood the bridle path led toward a farm about half a mile away. Not far from the farm we could see a large house with attached sheds.

'Who lives over there, in that farm?' inquired Holmes.

'That's the Long's farm on the right and the other is the Blanscome Stables,' replied Cartwright.

Holmes said, 'the thieves may have hidden your horse close by. I suggest, Superintendent that the horse could be in either of those two places over there. On the other hand, it may have been taken much further away. Perhaps, you will allow me to investigate alone. I will, of course, have to adopt a disguise.'

'Mr Holmes, I cannot believe that either Blanscome or Long has anything to do with my horse,' exclaimed Cartwright. 'We have been friends for many years.'

'Mr Cartwright,' replied Holmes, 'with any investigation I have to consider all possibilities. Now I suggest we return to your stables.'

When we arrived back at Cartwright's stables there was a letter waiting for him. Apparently it had been delivered by a boy from the village. He read it and handed to Holmes.

'Well, well. They are demanding that the five thousand guineas ransom be put in a small bag and placed on top of the Devil's Tooth and you are to wait there at noon tomorrow. If there is any sign of others nearby the collector will not arrive and you may never see your horse again,' said Holmes. 'Where and what is the Devil's Tooth?'

'On top of the downs not far from here close to a dew pond,' replied Cartwright. 'It's a large upright stone, four foot high, in the shape of a tooth. The once-pointed part has long been missing. It is supposed to date from the Stone Age and had some religious purpose.'

'Undoubtedly who ever wrote this is familiar with this part of the county and knows all about the Devil's Tooth and that a bag could be placed on the top,' commented Holmes.

'I assume that on top of the downs there are no bushes or trees we could hide behind?' said the superintendent.

'That is right, Superintendent. There is nowhere to hide,' replied Cartwright.

'Our next move, Superintendent,' said Holmes, 'is for Mr Cartwright to go to the stone at noon and place a bag on top. Had I not been as tall as I am I would have personated him and taken his place and endeavoured to arrest who ever arrives to collect the bag. I still do not understand why Mr Cartwright has to wait by the stone. Perhaps it will provide who ever intends to collect the money assurance that it is waiting to be collected.'

'Are you willing to go alone to the stone Mr Cartwright?' asked Shershay.

'Certainly. I doubt that they will want to harm me. All they want is the money.'

The owner went up to the Devil's Tooth in order to place the bag on top. When he returned he told us what has happened. 'I stood there for a few minutes. At first there was no one in sight. After a minute or two I became aware of a horse and rider that was trotting to and fro about a quarter of a mile from me. At first I did not take much notice. Only when the rider had changed direction once again did I begin to have a premonition that perhaps he had come to collect the bag. Before I fully realised what was happening he was coming at me at full gallop. I had to step aside as horse and rider swept past me. I saw then that the bag had been snatched up.'

'Were you able to observe any details of the horse or the rider?' asked Holmes. 'For example, did you recognise the horse, had it any particular markings? Was the rider wearing gaiters, riding boots and breeches or jodhpurs? What of his headgear?'

'Mr Holmes, I was so surprised at the speed with which everything happened that I regret I can recall little about either the horse or the rider other than he was masked.'

'As someone who is an experienced judge of a horse's movements, did you observe any peculiarity in the horse's gait as it came towards you? The reason I ask is to identify an animal that has some defect. Had there been then we may have been able to follow its hoof prints. Otherwise they will be little different from thousands of others to be found around here.'

'I could see nothing wrong with the way it was moving.'

Back at the stables Holmes asked to speak to the head lad. 'I need to put some questions about the attack on him which could provide clues to the identity of the thieves.'

'Jacob Waters is not here, Mr Holmes,' replied Cartwright. 'He has gone over to his sister's house over at Stoney Bottom. He told me that she had a remarkable remedy for bruises. I have to admit one side of his face was literally black and blue.'

'Oh, was it indeed? Most interesting. Has he been with you for some time?' asked Holmes.

'About two years. He was a successful jockey until he became too heavy for the weighing chair.'

Holmes then set out on his own to see if he could find any clues between where the horse had been seized, and the road that went past the farm and the other stables, in an attempt to find the horse. He changed into some borrowed clothes and partly disguised his prominent features. When he returned two hours later he announced, 'I have found your horse and it appears to be unharmed.'

'Oh, I am relieved Mr Holmes,' said Cartwright. 'Where is he?'

'In the paddock of the Blanscome Stables.'

'But, surely not. Blanscome would never do such a thing.'

'Nevertheless, one of the horses matches the description you gave me.'

Once Holmes had become Holmes again we set off for the Blanscome stables. The owner was most surprised to find a superintendent of Scotland Yard on his doorstep and even more surprised that someone who he had always assumed was a long standing friend should accuse him of stealing his horse.

'I have no idea what you are on about, Cartwright. You are accusing me of taking Son of Malvolio? Preposterous. How could you think such a thing of me? I have always been your friend.'

The superintendent said, 'Mr Blanscome, may I introduce the famous detective Mr Sherlock Holmes. He has found the horse in your paddock.'

'Of course it's not. Come and see for yourselves.'

He led us round to the paddock. It was a large field surrounded by trees and with a barn at one end. There were over two dozen horses grazing on the last of the autumn grass. From the top of the paddock, one could only see the heads and withers of some of those standing in the lower part. 'As these are all your horses, Mr Blanscome, I presume you are familiar with the markings and colour of each of them?' asked the superintendent.'

'Usually, but most of them only arrived two days ago. I have not had time to get to know them. I bought them at the Handcastle sale last week. Come on, I demand that you look at all of them. I should be most surprised if you find your horse Cartwright.'

He was astonished when Cartwright led us up to his horse and said. 'Superintendent, with great regret I must insist you charge Mr Blanscome with theft.'

At that point Holmes interjected, 'not so fast Mr Cartwright. If your friend had taken the horse I doubt that he would keep it here in the paddock. More than likely, if he were a thief, which I doubt, he would have hidden the animal somewhere else.

'I suppose so,' admitted Cartwright.

'I observed that the hedge in the corner of the paddock has been forced apart and there are hoof marks and footprints in the mud' said Holmes. 'Son of Malvolio was almost certainly led in through that way and not through the stable yard gate. If Mr Blanscome had taken the horse he would have taken it that way and not through the hedge. Furthermore, if Mr Cartwright will come with me to where his horse was forced through the hedge I will point out the impressions of its racing plates.'

Cartwright agreed that the impressions in the mud were those of his horse. After further discussion he accepted that

Blanscome was not guilty but did not understand why the horse had been put in his paddock.

Holmes explained. 'The thieves had to hide the horse somewhere. If they tried to keep it in a stable or shed a search of this part of the county would have eventually located it. Instead they hid it among two dozen or so other horses where its presence would not be noticed for some time. Time in which to win large sums on the Rockingham, or receive the ransom money in exchange. Perhaps both.'

'Mr Holmes, we now have to find the thieves,' said Shershay. 'I suspect that they are from this part of the county because they are obviously familiar with Mr Blanscome's stables and the neighbouring ones as well as all the farms. Have you discovered anything that will lead us to them?'

'Apart from the cravat pin, the florin and some items which I collected on my way along the path that leads to here, I have yet to reach any conclusions concerning the identity of those who took the horse. I suggest Mr Cartwright that you do not take your horse back to your stables until nightfall. The thieves may be waiting an opportunity to remove him after dark to somewhere else. Even though you have paid what they demanded they will not return your horse before the Rockingham. They may even demand more money for its return. We need to leave the trap set, as it were, so that they assume the horse is still where they had hidden it.'

'I agree with that plan, Mr Holmes. In the meantime I'll arrange with the local constabulary to provide a watch on the paddock,' said the superintendent.

After further discussion concerning the safety of Malvolio, we left and journeyed back to London. The closer our train came to its destination the more the tentacles of the spreading metropolis intruded on the once bucolic scenery. Villages, which were previously isolated and unknown, now had at least one villa owned by someone who previously had never set foot more than five miles from Charing Cross. I mused on the possible future of our great capital. 'Could there be any limit to its expansion? Might it extend one day to embrace all the Home Counties?' Then I turned my thoughts to the world of horse racing.

'Holmes, I was thinking about how you managed to find the horse so quickly. Why were you able to find the gap made in the hedge of the paddock?' I asked.

'Not a difficult test of observation, Watson. You will recall that the horse and rider were accosted late in the afternoon and sunset was approaching. The thieves had previously forced a gap in the paddock boundary and had marked the spot with a handkerchief stuck in the hedge. As I made my way along the path I saw the handkerchief. At first I though it had been lost by someone and that it had been blown by the wind against the hedge. However, when I looked closely I could see that it had been tied to the hedge. The thieves had intended that it would be dark when they brought the horse to the paddock and they needed to know where the gap was.'

'May I suggest that perhaps after all someone in the Blanscome stables, unknown to the owner, was part of the plot and had prepared the gap in the hedge and left the handkerchief as a sign?.'

'That thought had occurred to me. I have kept the handkerchief in the hope that it will provide an important lead to the criminals.'

'Does it in itself give any clue?'

'In a way it does.'

He showed me one corner where I could see the holes where the owner's initials had once been stitched on. 'If you look closely, Watson, you can just make out the initials JW. They could be yours.'

'JW could be Jacob Waters the head lad at the Cartwright stables. Could he be part of the conspiracy?'

'He could be. But we are looking for more than one thief. I am assuming that, if he is, he is not the instigator of the plot. One thing in particular concerning Waters is why has the monogram been unstitched? That is if the handkerchief is his. Oh, and something I forgot to tell you is that when I went along the bridle path following the hoof prints I came to spot underneath some trees where the thieves had stopped for some time. I concluded from the number of cigarettes that had been smoked that they had been there for about half an hour. Possibly they had been waiting until it was fully dark before attempting to lead the horse through the gap in the hedge.'

'Any particular cigarettes?' I asked.

'Indeed, among the discarded cigarette ends were those of a French brand, Aremis Bleu. Such a clue might lead one to surmise that all that needs to be done is find someone in the racing world who is either French or has lived or ridden as a jockey over there. Unfortunately their number could be in the hundreds.'

'Once again,' I said, 'you are faced with what to me appears to be an impossible task. I cannot see how you can proceed any further. You have so little to go on.'

'I have to admit, my dear fellow that I am not getting far with this horse affair. All that I have are a cravat pin, a florin, a handkerchief and the ends of French cigarettes and little else. The Rockingham is run in the next few days. Son of Malvolio was last quoted at two to one. Those who placed large bets a few days ago at long odds on the other favourites are likely to be disappointed if Malvolio wins.'

Our arrival at Waterloo station ended the discussion. Our concern now was how to find a hansom amid the dreadful muddle that was typical of one of the largest and busiest of London's termini. I have mentioned before that it was an insult to the Empire's capital to have, as one of its termini, a disparate collection of rambling low sheds, platforms whose system of numbering defied logic and parts of the station that gave the impression that they were nothing to do with their neighbouring groups of platforms.

As our hansom took us to Baker Street I removed from one of my pockets a cutting I remembered I had. 'Listen to this Holmes. I will read to you from this opinion on travelling by the railway that appeared in *Punch* a few years ago. Although it does not refer to Waterloo as such, nevertheless I think you will agree it is in accord with our own recent experience. It refers to stations in general and to their multiplication of steep slopes and precipitous staircases, the careful laying out of intricate passages and complicated corridors, the artful adjustment of numerous narrow wicket gates and the sedulously maintained mystery of many and capriciously used platforms.'

'Most apposite, Watson.'

Son of Malvolio was in time for the Rockingham. It won by a head. Presumably there were a number of villains who found they had put a lot of money on the wrong horse. A further visit was made to the Cartwright stables. Superintendent Shershay met us there. Previously, by telegram, we had asked Mr Cartwright to ensure that Jacob Waters was sent away on some pretext so that Holmes could examine his room.

'I need to be in the room alone so that I can study closely every detail,' said Holmes. I believe in *genius loci*. A few minutes contemplating the contents of a room often provides me with a mental picture of the life style and preferences of its occupant. Somewhere there has to be something, perhaps very small, that will lead me to the next step in this investigation.'

When he rejoined us ten minutes later he told us what he had observed in the room. 'I did find something that may lead further along the trail. For the moment I choose not to discuss it until I can be more certain of its validity. However, there was a small pocket book in which on most of the pages were written various amounts of money along with groups of figures which I deduce were betting odds. Waters appears to have spent and lost a lot of money on the horses. There was also a screwed up piece of paper at the back of one of the drawers. When I smoothed it out I could read a short note written from someone who threatened dire consequences if the amount owed was not paid immediately. Clues are more often than not difficult to come upon during an investigation; as we are all well aware. However, for once, a small piece of paper has provided a way forward without me having to make too much effort. Obviously JW is in debt and when someone in a stable is in debt the temptation to divulge information concerning horses is hard to resist. Also I have yet to find the reason why he should have a handkerchief from which the initials have been unstitched. During my investigation of the room I kept returning to the spots of ink that were on top of a chest of drawers where stood his wash basin and water jug. Had those spots been on the small table, where he most likely wrote in his notebooks, I could understand their presence.'

'A singular observation,' I suggested.

'Watson, do you recall that when we were talking to Mr Cartwright about the events on the day the horse was abducted, he mentioned that when Waters came into the stable yard, to say that he had been attacked and the horse stolen, his face exhibited a large blue black bruise?. As you will confirm, Watson, the distinctive colouration of a bruise does not manifest itself until some time after a blow has been received. I believe the bruise was in fact ink. I also believe he was not beaten by the thieves and neither was he tied up, because I found no trace of any rope fibres, let alone a discarded rope on the gallop. I am now certain that he was party to the theft. Recall that he was not present when we were at the stables. With some modesty, I can say that on hearing who I was he decided to keep away, knowing I would easily see through his deception.'

Cartwright listened to Holmes' deductions concerning his head stable lad. 'Mr Holmes,' he said, 'I now recall that around midday on the day of the theft I had to tell him not to air a saddle blanket by hanging it over the stable yard gate. He had never done such a thing before. Some time later I found the blanket still over the gate. By then he had taken Malvolio out onto the gallop. Could that have been a signal to the thieves?'

'More than likely,' replied Holmes. 'From a distance the thieves could see the blanket hanging over the gate probably as a signal that the horse was about to be exercised and also that no other horses and riders would be on the gallop at the same time.'

Waters returned to find a pair of handcuffs waiting for him. That, however, was not the end of the affair. Holmes still had to track down those who had taken the horse. A large reward put up by the racing authorities encouraged my friend to continue the chase even though it was not the sort of case, with the possible exception of Silver Blaze, in which he usually had much interest.

'There has to be a clue with the items I studied in Water's room,' said my companion after breakfast. It was few days after the visit to the racing stable and I had wondered when he would take up the case again.

'I took the liberty, Watson, of keeping the threatening letter that Waters had received. Some where in the make of paper, the ink, the handwriting and the manner in which it has been worded rests a clue that will enable me to take the next step. But what it is I have not the faintest idea. I am at a complete loss. Perhaps a morning of contemplation with my violin or some excellent strong tobacco may show me the way forward.'

Fortunately, at all times I had a ready reason to say that I had to visit a relative or make some purchase. I left while I was still able to find my way to the sitting room door. I went for a long walk in Regents Park during which I endeavoured to exercise my ability to determine the work, profession, health and degree of satisfaction with their lives of persons coming towards me.

When I entered the front door on my return I was alert for the sound of a violin and my nostrils for the aroma of tobacco smoke. I was pleased that there was neither. I found Holmes at the writing desk.

'Any progress with the horse case?' I asked.

'Perhaps there is. This scrap of paper with the threat to Waters indicates that the writer uses the Chancery Cursive hand.'

'Yes, I have heard of it. Come to think of it, the drawing master at my school endeavoured to introduce it but the headmaster insisted we persevere in perfecting a copperplate hand. But even though it is not in common use I anticipate that there must be a few thousand who do use it.'

'This is where, my dear chap, I have to depart from my own standards of investigatory procedure and take a chance or, rather, a guess. Something I am loath to do. Nevertheless I am going to assume that the writer of the letter is associated with the turf and furthermore has something to do with betting. On that basis the letter suggests that Waters is in debt to a bookmaker.'

'A reasonable assumption.'

'Among the different variations of the Chancery Italic Hand are those which have exaggerated ascenders and descenders. This particular writer uses both, on the letter P for example. The enclosed loop is attached to a long stroke that extends both above and below it. Most distinctive. Now if we were to be in the betting enclosure of one of the courses in Wessex there is the slight possibility that among the odds chalked on one of the bookmakers boards we will find such a letter P.'

'I see. But it would take us ages to visit all the courses and examine all the odds that have been marked up.'

'I agree, Watson. Therefore I am going to suggest to Shershay that an illustration is sent to every police station in the area. If at each race meeting there is a constable, provided with a copy of the illustration of the chancery letter P showing an extended ascender and descender, it would not take each constable long to examine all the bookmakers' boards.'

The superintendent agreed to Holmes' proposal and a few days later a telegram arrived announcing the name of a bookmaker at one of the Wessex courses. To mark up the odds on his board, he used a cursive hand with the Ps having a distinctive extended ascender and descender.

'We may have our man, Watson. Are you one for another venture westward?'

Despite my somewhat expensive interest in the Turf I cannot report that a wet blustery October day spent standing in among the crowd of punters and bookmakers was to my liking. Although I was pleased to be away from London's polluted atmosphere I would have preferred a more clement environment. I much preferred to wager from the comfort of the sitting room by taking advantage of that now ubiquitous and most useful device, the telegraph. Both my one-time injured shoulder and leg began to ache.

An inspector from the local constabulary met us and led us toward one of the bookmakers. We watched as he used his chalk to write up the odds he was offering. Despite the rapidity with which he wrote, erased and changed the odds there was no doubt that it was a Chancery hand he was using. There was the distinctive letter P with its exaggerated ascender and descender.

'I will go closer and make some observations,' said Holmes.

'Should I arrest him Mr Holmes?' asked the inspector.

'No, Inspector, it is too soon to make an arrest. It would only alert the others who were implicated in the stealing of Son of Malvolio.'

We watched as Holmes, pretending to be interested in the odds being offered, made a close study of the bookmaker's pitch. When he rejoined us I could tell he had discovered important evidence. 'Although it had been much trodden upon I was able to discern the remains of an Aramis Bleu,' said he. 'And that provides further confirmation that this suspect has a partner in crime who smokes that make of cigarette'.

During the journey back to London I raised the question of how it would be possible to find a smoker of Aramis Bleu among the thousands of people who attended horse races or were involved with horses and stables.

Holmes replied, 'I have thought of a way. I will send a telegram to every snuff, cigar and cigarette shop in Wessex. It will request the name or description of any customer who regularly purchases Aramis Bleu. I expect that there may be only one or two shops who stock or have heard of the brand. That in itself will help to narrow down the search.'

Back in Baker Street I helped Holmes with the task of determining from trade directories the names and addresses of the tobacconists in Wessex; one of whom might stock Aramis Bleu. Within three days a telegram arrived that provided both a place and a name. There were no other positive replies; most pointed out that there was little demand for such exotic cigarettes in that part of the kingdom. The positive reply had come from a tobacconist in Bishops Stonebridge, a market town, conveniently for us, on the South Western railway.

Holmes lost no time and the following day we journeyed to Bishops Stonebridge and arrived at the tobacconist who had replied that he stocked Aramis Bleu cigarettes. Superintendent Shershay had arranged for Inspector Ducket from the local constabulary to accompany us. After a number of questions had been posed by Holmes to the tobacconist it was established that he only had one customer who purchased the special cigarettes. Holmes then asked 'does the customer that buys Aramis Bleu come into your shop to collect them?'

'No, he sends a lad for them along with payment for the next month's supply that I order from a wholesaler in London.'

'Then he lives in the town?'

'Oh, no, I have never seen him around here. The boy usually arrives on a bicycle and, if I were a detective, I would surmise that he has come some distance.'

'Why do you say that?' asked Holmes.

'Because he is often puffed out and when it is raining he arrives soaked to the skin. Oh, and another thing I have noticed is that even if it is or has not been raining his trousers are wet up to his knees. And that could mean that he rode his bicycle through the ford which is at the bottom of this street.'

Holmes laughed and said, 'for a tobacconist, you make a good detective. What you have told us could be important. Ah, another thing, do you know his name?'

'He's a strange lad. I should have mentioned that he is a mute and no one seems to know where he lives or what his name is.'

At the police station Holmes studied an ordnance survey map of the district saying, 'Inspector Ducket, please point out the ford mentioned by the tobacconist.'

The inspector put his finger on the map. 'Just there, Mr Holmes, at the bottom of Haymarket street.'

'I suggest that what we must now do Inspector is cross the ford and find a trail that the lad usually took on his way back to where ever he lives. It might lead us to the smoker of French cigarettes.'

The inspector borrowed a trap and we set off down the hill. Once across the two or three feet depth of water we stopped to let Holmes examine the road that led upwards from the ford.

'He could go up the hill or turn left or right along the river bank,' said Holmes. 'Now, if we look at these tracks in the dried mud they clearly show that no one has ridden a bicycle along the river side; at least within the past week. Inspector, before we proceed up the hill why does the boy come this way when, as I saw on the map, there is a bridge downstream and a good class road that avoids one having to go up and over this ridge? Are there any dwellings between here and where this road joins the other one?'

'Only one, as far as I know, Mr Holmes. Betsy Fromely, a widow, lives there along with her chickens. She only comes into the town on market day to sell eggs. We will come to where the path to her cottage starts near the top.'

We set off up the steep hill, walking to save the horse.

As we neared the top Holmes advised the inspector to stop before we reached the point where the path led to the widow's cottage. He stood for a time contemplating the tracks in the dried mud.

'I can see that a cyclist has left the road and pushed his machine along the pathway. I can also see that he has come back and turned so as to continue along this road.'

'Is that significant?' asked the inspector.

'It could be,' replied Holmes. 'It provides an explanation to why he took this way and not the metalled road over the bridge. The widow might provide a clue. Although, for the present I shall just keep it in mind. It might be one of those baffling pieces of a jigsaw puzzle that you have to set on one side because there is no readily apparent place for it.'

Down the hill on the other side of the ridge we came to the metalled road.

'Which way, Mr Holmes? We may as well toss for it.'

'I understand games of chance, but I never proceed with an investigation that has to rely on chance. In this case we must apply logic.' Holmes pointed with his stick at the surface of the road. 'These tracks of a bicycle indicate that if it were those of the boy's machine then he turned right. Tell me, Inspector, are any of the dwellings to our right closer than any to our left?

'There's nothing, as far as I know to our left for another ten miles. To the right we will soon come to Plowright's farm.'

'This suggests that the boy either lives at Plowright's farm or at some other place between there and the bridge. What do you know of Mr Plowright?'

'Not much. Keeps to himself. Never been seen in the town. Gossip has it that he was once a clergyman. He was defrocked following despicable and scandalous affairs in his parish.'

We turned right and soon came on the farm.

'Yes, that's Plowright's place,' said the inspector. 'I'll go in and see what I can find.'

'No, Inspector. Better that we stay back and watch,' suggested Holmes. 'Otherwise, if the smoker of French cigarettes is in there he will be warned that he is being investigated and more than likely run off.'

From a secluded place among the trees at the side of the road we kept watch. Eventually our patience was rewarded and a boy arrived on a bicycle. We continued to study the farm. There was little activity until we saw two men enter the yard and start to examine a horse. Both wore rough clothing and gave the appearance of farmers. Suddenly Holmes whispered to me, 'Watson, look at the taller of the two. Thin, over six feet, smoking a slim cigar. Can you see his sharp features? Does he not remind you of Tresscot-Jones?'

I could see what Holmes meant. It could be that villain of the Deerstalker affair and the one who on another occasion tried to kill both Holmes and myself.

I replied, 'it could be him.'

'Do you know the gentleman, Mr Holmes?' asked Inspector Ducket.

'We do indeed. We have both had occasions to cross his path. The last time was a close run thing,' replied Holmes. 'He escaped from Dartmoor about six months ago and disappeared.'

'As he is an escaped convict then I can enter the premises without a warrant and arrest him. Look, they've gone inside the house.'

'Are you armed, Inspector?'

'I have never had the need to be in these parts,' he replied.

'Then it is fortunate that both Dr Watson and I carry pistols. Frequently during my investigations we come up against villains who will only surrender if they are faced with a gun.'

We decided to split up. Holmes went into the yard and through the door leading into the house. I was detailed to go round to the other side of the house and see if I could effect an entrance. Fearful that I might suddenly come upon Tresscot-Jones, I gripped my revolver in my shaking and sweating hand and proceeded as quietly as I could. An open window provided the obvious way in for me. I put my gun on the window ledge and heaved myself up. No sooner had my head passed through when an arm locked round my neck. I was trapped. A voice, the voice I dreaded to hear, that of Tresscot-Jones, said, 'well, well, it's Dr Watson, that other meddling investigator.'

I was well and truly trapped. I managed to make one shout for help before a hand was clamped over my mouth. I was about to succumb to the pressure on my windpipe when I heard Holmes shout, 'leave him, you devil.' I fell back out of the window. A gun fired, then another shot. When I recovered my senses I looked into the room. Holmes stood, gun in hand. Sprawled away from the window was the villain who had nearly finished me off. Holmes, in a most remarkably calm voice, said, 'I've only winged him. I have to admit to poor shooting on my part. However, he will continue to enjoy hard labour on Dartmoor for many more years.'

The inspector came into the room and handcuffed the groaning villain who had been hit in the thigh by a bullet from Holmes' gun.

His companion, Plowright, the unfrocked priest, made no attempt to join the affray. The contents of the farm house revealed that, despite his modest appearance, Plowright was a rich man. Examination of what was obviously his study, or rather office, showed that he was the master mind behind a crooked gambling organisation that employed all kinds of tricks to defraud those who bet on horses as well as the bookmakers. We also found many packets of Aramis Bleu cigarettes as well as a supply of cheroots. The cigarette ends on the ground, where the kidnappers of Son of Malvolio had waited, was sufficient evidence to show that he had been there at the time. Although it could not be proved, we were certain that the rider who snatched the bag from the top of the Devil's Tooth was Tresscot-Jones. We also found the mute and his bicycle. The widow who lived alone in a cottage on the top of the ridge proved to be the boy's mother. That explained why he took the more difficult route between the farm and the town. We also found evidence that confirmed that the bookmaker who wrote a particular shape of the letter P was a partner in crime with Plowright and Tresscot-Jones.

When reviewing the case a thought came to my mind.

'Holmes, what of the ink spots you observed in the stable lad's room?'

'Ah, yes, a good question. The answer is simple. He had soaked a sponge or small cloth in ink with which to dye his face to make it appear to have been bruised. He had taken it with him when he set off to exercise the horse.'

'Another thing, Holmes, how did you deduce so quickly that the owner of the horse was from the racing world?'

'Not difficult, old chap, he put his hat upside down on the table and I could read the hatter's label inside the band. It was that of an establishment in Lambourne which, as I am sure you know, is surrounded by many racing stables. Furthermore, his cravat pin was formed with two crossed whips.'

As for the cravat pin found on the gallop, it remained unclaimed. The discarded cigarettes proved to be the most important clue in the affair of a horse that was stolen and then quickly recovered. And, of course, this was our third confrontation with Moriarty's protégée.

THE END

THE CHEVEREUX LETTER

In which Sherlock Holmes has to investigate a seemingly 'watertight' alibi and the location of jewellery hidden by Mary Queen of Scots.

I had been acting for two weeks as locum to a friend who had a practice in the provinces. On my return to 221B Baker Street I was anxious to hear from Holmes of any investigations with which he had been involved while I was away.

'In answer to your question, my dear Watson, I have to say I have had a rather dull existence. Only one case has come to my attention.'

'Is it a murder?'

'No. There is no body and no vicious assaults. It just concerns a painting by Rubens which has been stolen from a Tudor mansion in Barnet, owned by Simon de Chevereux, an aged recluse. When the servants of the house were questioned they suggested that William, a nephew of the owner, might have been searching for a letter. The letter was supposed to have been written by that unhappy queen, Mary Stuart, and it may have been hidden behind the canvas of the painting.'

'A letter written by the Queen of Scots, you say.'

'Yes, it is believed she wrote a letter disclosing where the greater part of her jewellery had been hidden in one of the different houses in which she had been confined on the orders of her cousin Elizabeth. According to the family history, on the day before she was removed to Fotheringay Castle and her

150

eventual execution, she gave a letter to Sir Roger de Chevereux, her keeper. The letter is purported to say that he was to have the treasure in recognition of his kindness to her and the comfortable manner in which she had been confined in his house'

'Which means that somewhere in the house in Barnet is an historic letter.'

'Possibly.'

'I think all this has the making of an intriguing tale.'

'That will depend on whether there ever was such a letter. Succeeding generations of the family have searched for it. Apparently, the house has been scoured most thoroughly on a number of occasions over the centuries that have passed. Walls have been opened up, wainscoting and flooring removed. All the likely hiding places in a Tudor house have been searched but to no avail. Sir Roger died a month after the queen's execution. He may have bequeathed the letter, if it existed, to his eldest son or made a dying statement concerning the location of the jewels.'

'Is the theft of the painting of interest to you?

'Not particularly, but Shershay of the Yard appears to be baffled by the unshakeable alibi presented by the nephew, William, who is the principal suspect. He has asked for my help.'

'Did you visit the house?'

'I did but I cannot say that I was able to find anything which could positively indicate that the nephew had been there at the night of the robbery.'

'Is it a large painting with a heavy frame? I only ask because, surely, the thief would have found it difficult to carry away.'

'Yes, it is large but it was cut from the frame. From my conversations with the servants I gathered that who ever took it may have been looking behind the canvas for the queen's letter. The facts as we know them, Watson, definitely point to the nephew because he appears to be the most likely one to have stolen it. I have to say likely and not positively, because all we have to go on is the confused recollection of Simon de Chevereux that he saw his nephew, or imagined it was he in the room that night. He may have called out to him. When I questioned the servants they told me that their master often said he had visitors both during the day and at night when, in fact, there had been none. William the nephew has now been released from custody because of a lack of positive evidence and his seemingly sound alibi for the time of the theft. While he was in custody the police searched his house in Islington but the painting was not found.'

'As you have often reminded us, Holmes, alibis can be unsound however plausible they seem at first.'

'Indeed. But in this case the nephew has provided the police with the names of three people close to where he lives who could vouch that he had been with them at the time of the theft.'

As we sat before the fire that evening and after conversation between us had been exhausted, my mind turned to the

Chevereux case. I went over the facts and in particular the scene of the crime, as described by Holmes.

I imagined the old recluse seated before a dying fire late at night. All but his manservant had gone to bed. All the candles had finished their course and, away from the circle of light cast by the fire, the room was a confusion of shadows. The old man was accustomed to the gloom. His mind was full of memories: so much so that the boundary between what was real and what was imagined was indistinct. A shadow often appeared to him as a person. Some by the flickering light of the fire appeared to move. Anyone younger and with a vivid imagination might have become terrified at what the old man sometimes greeted as relatives or old friends. That night one of the shadows was more distinct than others. It moved. The recluse stirred in his chair and said, 'William, is that you? Why have you come to see your uncle so late?' The shadow did not respond and moved away from the light. The dull sound of a knife cutting canvas in a far corner of the room went unheard by the recluse. His mind had already forgotten the apparition of his nephew.

The next morning our breakfast was disturbed by the arrival of Superintendent Shershay of the Yard. 'Good morning Gentlemen. My apologies for disturbing you so early in the day.'

'No matter. Dr Watson and I have just finished breakfast. Perhaps you might like some toast. We have recently received a most excellent marmalade from Dorset.'

'Most kind of you Sir, but no thank you. Can we discuss the alibi of William de Chevereux?'

'Certainly. On the face of it, it might be an acceptable alibi,' replied Holmes.

153

'Perhaps if you were to talk to him you might detect some inconsistency in his account of where he was on the night of the theft.'

I always found the relationship between my friend and the police detectives most interesting. The latter gave the impression that they considered Holmes' methods of investigation rather fantastical and theoretical. On one occasion I overheard one of them voice the opinion that my friend had the makings of a good detective!

Later in the day we went with the superintendent to William de Chevereux's house. It was one in a row which I believe is described as shabby-genteel. In response to a knock, the door was opened by a woman of uncertain age, modestly dressed and having an air of someone none too pleased to see the superintendent again. I was certain that within a minute Holmes had gathered from the woman's appearance and manner the history of her life. We were shown into a room on the table of which was the remains of a meal. Holmes took charge of the conversation and questioned the suspect about where he had been and with whom he had conversed on the night of the crime. I observed that William de Chevereux was about twenty years of age. His appearance suggested that he was a reasonably well-paid clerk; perhaps in a solicitor's office. He insisted he had spent the greater part of the night of the robbery attempting to win at a game of cards with friends. That is what he had told the police.

The nephew clung to his story and we left him. On the way back to Baker Street we discussed the interview.

'Mr Holmes, have you come to any conclusion about the young man's alibi?' asked the superintendent.

'It certainly has the appearances of being a good one,' replied Holmes. 'I consider that among questions we need to answer are the following. Could he have left the card game and committed the crime without his companions being aware of his absence? I think not. Could those who have vouched for him be mistaken? Unlikely. Could he have misled them to the time of their encounters? Again, most unlikely. Which means we have to find another way of testing his alibi.'

'What do you suggest, Mr Holmes?' asked the superintendent.

'I will have to apply some careful thought to the problem. Perhaps I shall be able to give you an answer tomorrow.'

'What was your impression of our suspect, Mr Holmes?'

'I am sure we all agree that William's manner was markedly defensive and his wife appeared rather concerned at our presence and the questions we put to him. What did you think of his answers, Watson?'

'Plausible,' I replied. 'However, I observed that when you asked him if he had lived abroad he stiffened as if the question was not one he wanted to have to face. I recall he replied, "Certainly not, why do you ask." You said, "oh, no particular reason." One thing I must say is that I was aware of the perspiration on his forehead and the trembling of his hands.'

Our conversation moved on to other aspects of the interview.

The next day at breakfast I was having difficulty eating bacon and eggs with one hand; having badly sprained my right wrist two days previously. I had to cut the bacon with my left hand.

'Mrs Hudson should have cut your bacon up into small pieces,' commented Holmes.

A few minutes later he suddenly banged the table. 'Of course, of course. I have just remembered.' he exclaimed. 'There may have been a third person in the house or one who had just left before we arrived.

'Ah, but there were only two sets of plates and cutlery on the table.'

'Just so. But what we do not know is whether or not William was the one who had used the plate that was in front of him. He happened to be sitting at that place when we entered. Or, he contrived to move there when he heard his wife open the door to us. All this leads me to consider the possibility of an American living there or one who had just visited there.'

'Why do you say it could be an American? Surely, my dear fellow, you cannot detect the nationality of someone you have never met, let alone seen? I have always accepted without question your outstanding ability to determine someone's profession, their place in society and the health of their bank account. But this time you are stretching my belief somewhat.'

'Although I may not be absolutely certain of the nationality of the third possible occupant of the nephew's house, nevertheless there were a number of things I observed the moment we entered the dining room. They were of great significance.'

'Holmes, if, as you say, an American is or has been in the house he could just be a lodger.'

'Then why did they not mention it and why did the police, when they searched the house, not find traces of a lodger, such as clothing,'

'Are you suggesting, Holmes, that he is involved with de Chevereux?

'A possibility, yes.'

'Then we have to go again to the house with the superintendent and demand to see the third man. That is if there is a third man.'

'No, let us leave him for the time being but watch the house.'

The next day we were in the front room of a house opposite that of William de Chevereux. It was vacant and we had obtained the keys as prospective tenants. Our vigil was rewarded within an hour when, having watched William leave earlier, who should emerge from the house but someone who, at first sight, looked like William.

'The third man, the one you say is an American,' I suggested.

'Yes that's him,' replied Holmes. 'As I suspected, we may have another case of a double being used to commit a crime and to confuse any investigation by the police or even by me.'

'What is our next step, Mr Holmes?' asked the superintendent.

'Perhaps, Superintendent, a perusal of birth certificates at Somerset House may throw some light on the mystery.'

The superintendent returned to the yard, and Holmes departed for Somerset House. Holmes returned from his search to give me the information that two boys, Arthur and William, had been born on the same day to the nephew's mother.

'Well that seems to settle the matter. Both must be charged with theft,' I opined.

'I doubt it is as simple as that, Watson. If both men were in the dock their defence counsels would argue that the only witness to the theft, the uncle, could not have been certain which of the twins he saw that night. Even if he were to appear in the witness box for the Crown, defence counsel would have little difficulty in convincing a jury that his mind, sight and hearing were so impaired that he could have been mistaken. No, we have to proceed toward establishing, without doubt, it was Arthur, the other twin, who entered the house. The alibi submitted by William would certainly convince a jury. Nevertheless, I will wire the superintendent a summary of the conclusions I have reached so far. It should prove sufficient to arrest the twins.'

'What appears to be the end of the affair, Holmes, only proves to be the start of a further investigation.'

'Indeed. Not only have we got to clarify who is who but also find the Rubens. The twins have hidden it somewhere and I doubt that they were foolish enough to conceal it in William's house. It is extremely valuable and most likely by now has been sold to a fence.'

Fortunately for the case, one of Holmes' many links with the world of crime, which often provided important information, led to the Rubens portrait. It was seized by the police. Holmes decided he would like to see the painting. We went to a well known restorer of pictures who had been charged by Simon de Chevereux to clean it, and we examined the painting at the restorer's studio. The careful cleaning process to remove the layers of grime, accumulated over the years, was partly completed. Holmes looked closely at the portrait. The restorer said, 'Mr Holmes, there is something strange about this painting. If you look at the bottom right hand corner, where I have cleaned down to the original surface, there is an area where the paint is of a later date than that of the original.'

'I understand that changes and additions are often to be found when old paintings are restored,' said Holmes.

'Yes, quite often,' replied the restorer. 'Sometimes it is because of the need to repair damage to the canvas or the surface of the paint, or even because someone has wanted to delete an area containing a person or objects no longer considered acceptable.'

'Most interesting. Now this corner,' Holmes pointed to the recently cleaned area. 'I can discern through your splendid magnifying glass a house and under it a sea shell.'

'You are right. I doubt that they were painted by Rubens.'

On the next occasion when we were discussing the de Chevereux case Holmes said, 'I have given much thought to the painting, Watson, would you agree that the house and the sea shell that were added at a later date might be a subtle indication of the whereabouts of the queen's jewels?'

'You amaze me dear fellow. I would never have thought of such an idea.'

'Of course I may be completely wrong. All I would conjecture, at the present, is that the house depicted is where the jewels were hidden. As for the sea shell I will have to think about its possible meaning. You know, music can provide a refreshing draught to the mind. There is a Sarasate violin recital this evening and that is where I will be.'

As I have mentioned, my clever friend had many interests. He was an accomplished violinist and composer.

Another breakfast with Holmes was accompanied by a telegram. 'Listen to this Watson, the picture restorer tells me he has just cleaned another part of the Rubens and revealed what he thinks is yet another area that may have been painted over later.'

We lost no time in getting to the restorer.

'What have you found?' asked Holmes.

'Just here Mr Holmes,' replied the restorer. 'See, this depiction of a letter lying on the table under de Chevereux's pointing finger. I am certain it was not on the original. Please use the glass.'

'A most singular addition. If it is a later change. Have a look Watson.' I examined the letter through the proffered magnifying glass and could just make out the writing.'

'It seems to me it is in French, although some of the words are spelt in a peculiar way,' said I.

'Can you read the word that is directly under the pointing finger?'

Gradually I was able to make out the word.

'I can just see the word 'puits,' said I.

'That means a well or wells,' added the restorer.

Holmes gave an elated cry. 'Of course, the jewels are down a well at the house with the shell.'

After profuse thanks to the restorer we left.

The same evening Holmes curled himself up in his favourite chair and amid a cloud of tobacco smoke, busied himself with the volumes which provided the history and the arms of the noble families. It was some time before he exclaimed, 'Watson, I may have found the queen's jewels. They are more than likely at Halecroft the home of the Lefeyette family who are distant cousins of the de Chevereux. The arms of Lefeyette include a sea shell in recognition that one of them, a devout Catholic, had made the pilgrimage to Santiago in Spain.'

'I have to say, Holmes, a most satisfactory conclusion. Was there ever a letter?'

'I doubt it. The descendents of Roger de Chevereux have, over the years, believed that such a letter existed when in fact it was just imagined. The whereabouts of the jewels could have been passed down by word of mouth. However, at some time, for some unaccountable reason, it was decided to add information onto the painting of Sir Roger's son which could lead to the discovery of their whereabouts. If the Rubens had not been cleaned and you had not detected the French word for well we may still be trying to solve the mystery. As for the twins that is a matter for the law.'

'This is certainly a complicated case,' I remarked.

'Not really. Let me summarise what we have learned.'

Holmes leant back in his battered old chair, steepled his fingers to hold a long clay pipe and in a cloud of tobacco smoke began his summary.

'We now know from questioning Arthur de Chevereux that he had been taken to the United States by his mother when he was only a baby. Only recently had he read about the Rubens painting. That stirred his memory of something his mother had told him a few years back. She had told him about Mary Stuart and the bequest to his ancestor Sir Roger de Chevereux in recognition of his kindness to her; even though he was, in effect, her jailer. The treasure was not hidden in the Chevereux house but in another of the many houses into which the queen had been confined. Before she left for Fotheringay castle she may have told Sir Roger where the jewels had been hidden. Arthur's mother had told him that there might be a letter at the back of the Rubens. Apparently, she had discovered, when packing her things for the journey across the Atlantic, an old piece of paper at the back of a drawer in one of the Tudor items of furniture in the Chevereux house. This had the cryptic message, "Rubens keeps what we have always sought."

'I suppose, Watson, the most important thing that I recalled after the visit to William's house was the meal on the table that had just ended before we arrived. I noted that the plate in front of William still had some meat on it but only the fork. The knife with traces of food on the blade lay beside the plate on the cloth. At the time I did not think that to be of importance. It was only when you had difficulty in eating your breakfast one handed did I suspect that an American was in the house or had just left. They often cut up their meat first and then just use the fork. I have questioned this practice but have yet to be told of its origin.'

'I was not aware of such a habit.'

Holmes continued his summing up. 'Three hundred years or more after the Scottish queen was executed Arthur de Chevereux decided to come to England to find his long lost brother. Together they plotted to seize the painting and hoped also to find an ancient document behind the canvas. You may ask, of course, why did they not go straight to their uncle and tell him what they knew. The answer lies again with family feuds. The twins' father had quarrelled with his brother over the inheritance on the death of their grandfather. The present, aged de Chevereux refused to quit the family home and did little to help his younger brother. However, he had on occasions allowed his nephew William to visit the house and stay for a day or two. This meant that when Arthur decided to seize the letter William was able to describe in detail where the painting was hung.'

'The alibi presented by William was sound. He spent most of the night in the company of friends who had known him for some years. While he was playing cards Arthur stole into the Chevereux house and cut the Rubens portrait out of its frame. Whether he hoped to find a letter or document hidden behind the canvas we do not know. Perhaps in finding none he decided to take the canvas and sell it.'

The twins were tried for theft. The Crown had little difficulty in convincing the jury that both were guilty; even though my friend was not called to give evidence.

When the painting was restored to its frame and back on the wall, where it had hung for four centuries, Holmes' bank account received a welcome addition. The story did not end there because some months later I found myself reading about a protracted argument in the courts over who was the legitimate owner of the jewels that had been discovered down a well.

My strained wrist and a knife had led to the solution of another investigation which I have had the pleasure to record.

THE END

THE BARRED DOOR PUZZLE

In which Sherlock Holmes determines if the death of a college professor was a case of suicide in a locked room, or murder.

As I have often recounted, the investigations and adventures of my friend Sherlock Holmes have commenced at the breakfast table with the arrival of a telegram or a visitor. However, this tale starts in the tea room at Liverpool Street station. We were passing the time before our train left for Cambridge by drinking coffee. I took advantage of the view from the top of the stairway leading from the West Side concourse to watch the comings and goings of the Great Eastern trains with their splendidly painted blue locomotives.

My companion was using his powers of observation to sharpen his ability to determine a person's character, occupation, state of health and, sometimes, the health of their finances. Below was a throng of potential candidates for his skilful occupation. From time to time he would draw my attention to a particular man or woman and provide me with information about them.

'Watson, you see that man of the cloth at the foot of the stairs?'

'Yes, he was sitting near us just now.'

'I am certain his is an impoverished parish. Note how his…' At that moment a voice interrupted his explanation. 'If I'm not mistaken its Sherlock Holmes.'

'Oh, of course, it's James Redding,' was Holmes' response. 'What a coincidence we should meet here. We are on our way to Cambridge. May I introduce my great friend and companion Doctor John Watson.' To me he said, 'Sir James Redding is Master of St Edmunds.'

We learned that Sir James was on his way back to Cambridge after attending business concerned with land which had been bequeathed to the college. Once our train was on its way we three discussed a number of topics of general interest, among which was that of Professor Sylvanus Thommason of St Edmunds who, apparently, had committed suicide.

'The death of Thommason has cast a shadow over the college,' said Sir James. 'You remember him, Holmes, do you not?'

'I do. He was extremely helpful to me when I went up. I read in the papers about his death. There was mention of doubt on the part of the police as to whether it was suicide.'

'That is so.' responded Sir James. 'The poor fellow was found with a gun in his hand slumped in his chair and a bullet wound to his temple. The inspector of police confided to me that he had doubts about the case and the coroner had postponed his verdict. This is a sad affair and I wish it could be settled.'

'Do you have confidence in the local police?' asked Holmes.

'I regret to say not. We have had a few cases of petty theft within the college and it became clear that the resources of the detectives, both mental and material, were limited.'

Nothing more was said on the subject for a time. I watched the fields and hedgerows spin by as if they were on the surface of a giant horizontal wheel. My thoughts turned to the reason why Holmes and I were on our way to Cambridge. I was looking forward to a change of scenery by accepting the invitation from my sister to stay with her family, and at the same time act as locum to her husband who had to attend a medical conference in Cardiff. Holmes had accepted the invitation to accompany me as it coincided with his wish to conduct chemical experiments in the Coburg Laboratory.

My reverie was broken by hearing Sir James saying to my friend, 'Holmes, forgive me if I am imposing on you but is there any way you could help with resolving the question of poor Thommason's death.'

'Of course, I would be most anxious to help,' was the reply. 'Mind you I have committed the Coburg Laboratory to giving me time for some experiments. Let me consider my answer when I have visited the laboratory and determined how much time can be allowed for other activities. I am sure I will be able to give some help.'

'I should be most grateful to you, Holmes.'

On arriving at my sister's house we were also unexpectedly greeted by her husband who informed us that the medical conference in Cardiff had had to be postponed because of a severe outbreak of cholera. My help was no longer needed. That meant I had more time for leisure and for exploring the ancient university town and, as it transpired, time to accompany Holmes as he investigated the death of the professor.

The next morning a letter arrived at breakfast indicating that Sir James had convinced the local police that Holmes' help could be of value. And so we started this new case with a visit to the police station where we met an Inspector Nokes. He was, in appearance and manner, another Lestrade. In other words a 'sharp-faced, keen-eyed' member of the detective force who would be quick and energetic, but tended to be conventional in the way in which he set about solving a problem.

After Holmes had introduced himself and explained the reason for our visit the inspector responded, 'Mr Holmes, this is an honour. We have often read of your exploits and I am certain you can help us to decide between suicide and murder in the case of Professor Thomasson.'

'I will do my best. May I introduce Doctor Watson? He is always a great help to me. If you have no objection I wish that he joins us.'

'None what so ever. Now I suggest we go to the mortuary as I am sure that is where you would want to start your investigation.'

'I agree,' said Holmes.

At the mortuary we examined the corpse. Holmes paid particular attention to the fatal wound to the temple. 'Do you not agree Watson that the bullet has passed right through the skull and emerged the other side?'

'Yes there is an obvious entry point and an exit.'

'Inspector, has the bullet been recovered?

'We could not find it, Mr Holmes.'

'In the meantime, please may I have sight of your notes? I need time to study them.'

'Certainly.'

Holmes took the notes written by the inspector back to my sister's house and without stopping for refreshment he began a careful perusal of them.

The next day, as arranged, the inspector took us up to the professor's room so that Holmes could study the scene of the crime.

'You say in your preliminary report, Inspector, that the victim was slumped in his chair with the gun still in his right-hand,' said Holmes.

'Yes, that is how he was when I arrived.'

'And there was no sign of a struggle or that any of the drawers or cupboards had been ransacked.'

'It is much as you see it now, Mr Holmes. I have read some of your writings on detective work and endeavoured to follow what you advise. I have tried to leave the room as I found it.'

'Good, I am pleased to hear it. Watson, you were right to encourage me to set down in print just a few of my methods. Of course I have not included anything that might provide criminals with knowledge that could help them with their illegal activities.'

As I anticipated, during his examination of the room Holmes went down on all fours and with his large magnifying glass studied parts of the floor and carpets. For a few minutes he said nothing. He just stood looking at a large chest of drawers that was positioned to one side. Then he asked, 'Inspector this chest of drawers has been moved at some time. Is it back in its usual position?'

'Yes it is, Mr Holmes. I questioned the servants and they confirmed that this is where it usually stands. It had been moved to block the door. Those who heard a shot and were concerned for the professor had great difficulty in pushing it away.'

'Now, what about the fireplace. I see that the grate has not been cleared.'

'As I told you, I ordered that nothing should be moved or touched.'

'Good. Ah, what have we here?'

Holmes held up a screwed up sheet of paper that he had found in the coal scuttle. He smoothed it out and studied it for a minute or two. 'Now this is interesting. It is obviously the last page of a letter sent to the Dean. I will read it. He writes: "*As you see, this is a serious business. He will not admit to his action despite my pleading. To think that a winner of the McClusky Prize should have stooped so low. Now we will have to find another candidate for the Chair of that name. I am sure you will appreciate, Dean, that this affair grieves me deeply.*" 'It is signed Thommason. I conclude this was either a draft, or the professor had second thoughts on the subject. What it does tell us is the name of the person to whom the professor is referring. It is he who won the McClusky Prize.'

'And who is that?' I asked.

'The Senior Tutor, Dr James Aspinoll.'

With the agreement of Sir James, the Master, Holmes interviewed some of Thomasson's contemporaries and we then took our leave.

Back at my sister's house Holmes began a further study of the inspector's notes.

'Holmes have you now reached any conclusions in the case?' I asked.

'For the time being, not many. All I am certain of is that the victim could not have shot himself because there were no powder burn marks on the skin surrounding the fatal wound. Only if there had been burn marks would it indicate that the gun might have been fired by him.'

'Then it is definitely murder.'

'No doubt of it.'

'Yet the door to the room was barred by an oak chest of drawers and the only way for the murderer to flee was through the window. When we examined the outside of the building we could find no drain pipes or architectural features that would have enabled someone to descend safely from the third floor.'

'Yes, that was at first a seemingly difficult matter to solve. Inspector Nokes told us that a search had been made for a long ladder; in fact one with a reach of at least thirty feet, which could have been abandoned close by. Even had they found such a ladder it would have proved difficult to reconstruct how, when carrying it, the villain could have gained entrance past the college porter; especially at that time of the night when he was making sure the undergraduates, in particular, were not attempting to introduce unauthorised persons to their rooms. Furthermore, I paid special attention to the window ledges and the window frames as well as the adjacent carpet. I could not find any signs that someone had attempted either to enter or leave the room through a window.'

'When I consider the facts I was at first inclined to suggest that a rope ladder was used. However, it would have had to be rather long and even when coiled up it would have been too big to avoid the eagle eye of the porter,' I ventured.

'I agree, Watson, a rope ladder would have been difficult to use let alone hide. I suspect a premeditated murder, in which the assassin had made a careful plan which included a method of leaving the room without having to pass through a window or a door.'

'Does that suggest a student or even an academic was the murderer and not someone from outside the college?' I opined.

'I am inclined to such a view. I suppose a singular clue were the marks made on the linoleum by the four feet of the chest of drawers.'

'Yes, I remember you spent some time on all fours studying the marks.'

'An uncomfortable position but rewarding. I saw that two of the feet had made wide sweeping marks whereas the other two feet had only moved a short distance. I was able to distinguish those marks from those made when the chest was pushed back to its usual place. I could see that the chest had been swung away from the wall where it usually stood. However, it had not been slid sideways across the door, which is what one would have expected if the victim had moved it before shooting himself. No, someone came into that room, shot the professor and then moved the chest so that it barred the door. It was done

172

to suggest suicide by indicating that the victim did not want anyone interrupting him.'

'And then the murderer left. But how?'

'Indeed, how? As we determined, it was most unlikely that after moving the chest he had escaped through the window and reached the ground safely.'

For a few minutes Holmes busied himself with charging and lighting a pipe. He curled up in a chair and appeared lost in thought. Suddenly he rose and began pacing up and down, leaving a trail of ash for the eventual chagrin of my poor sister, to whom subsequently I had to offer profuse apologies. Finally he stopped and said, 'Watson, I am dismissing entirely any idea of ladders and ropes. What happened is nothing more complex than the murderer shooting the professor, placing the gun in the victim's hand and leaving by the door. He then contrived to move the chest so as to confuse any investigation.'

'As you say, that seems to be what occurred. However, although I may be wrong in what I am going to say, I do not understand why the murderer took the trouble, as you determined, to swing the chest across the door and not just slide it across.'

'Watson, of course you are right to ask such a question. However, I am deliberately not replying to it because I have to give further thought to how the chest was moved.'

'Am I now right in assuming that the murderer never left the college, because the porter swore no one left that night? He also told us that there were no doors or windows on the ground floor that could be opened at night; so no one could leave other than by the main gate,' I said.

'A correct assumption, Watson. Now we come to the important fact that, as I learned, the professor was one of those few who displayed selective lateral preferences. I mean someone who is neither predominately right-handed and -footed for most activities but, for example, writes with their right-hand but plays cricket and tennis with the left.'

'The gun was in his right-hand according to the inspector.'

'Yes. From conversations with those who knew the professor well I realised the murderer may have been unaware that his victim only used his right-hand for writing. When he played cricket or tennis, which he frequently did, he used his left hand and, therefore, would most likely have held a gun in that hand. Which, of course, provides us with an important clue as to the identity of the murderer. All we have to do is to determine the sporting activities of likely suspects. If they play neither cricket nor tennis then their lack of knowledge of the professor's handedness may help to build a case against them.'

'I do not follow your reasoning. What would the fact someone does not play cricket or tennis have to do with the case?'

'Consider, my dear fellow, if they played either of those two games they would more than likely have played against the professor and thus been aware of his hand preference for activities requiring eye and hand coordination.'

'Obviously, you have put your finger on an important fact. Now may I make a suggestion?'

'Of course, I always value highly your opinions.'

'It is this. Did the murderer put the gun in the wrong hand in an attempt to confuse us?'

'That is also a possibility, Watson.'

'Can we be certain as to the time of the murder?'

'According to the inspector's notes some in the college did hear a shot but could not be certain as to the exact time. Comparing the statements about time I conclude that it was about half past nine. I also read that when three members of the college heard the shot they were not certain where the sound came from. The few who were in the vicinity rushed up the stairs and, according to them, Aspinoll was just ahead of them. They found the outer door open but could not at first open the door from the lobby into the professor's study. All we know is that Aspinoll visited the professor at half past eight carrying a viola case. No one saw him leave so we cannot set a time. At about half past nine a gun shot was heard.'

During the time required by Holmes to smoke two pipe-fulls of tobacco he said nothing. I did not interrupt because I was certain he was going over all the facts in the case and would soon announce who the murderer was and why he acted as he did. I was going over in my mind what I was intending to say to my bank manager on our return to the capital. Before we left London I had received a letter composed in the most polite terms pointing out that what was going into my account failed to keep pace with what was going out. I was considering how I would address this matter when Holmes interrupted my thoughts, 'Watson, can you recall on which floor stood a large basket from the steam laundry?'

'Well, yes, I am sure it was at the bottom of the stairs leading to the professor's room. Why do you ask?'

'Oh, just something that has come to mind. For the time being I prefer to delay my answer.'

'I noted that the police took the gun away. What do they intend to do with it?'

'A good question. I doubt they have the means for determining to whom it belongs and when it was last fired. Even the Scotland Yard detectives are no better served with proper forensic equipment. I sent them a copy of my guide to analysing weapons which have been used in the commission of crimes. I received no acknowledgment. I suspect they consider me an amateur in such matters and resent the involvement of members of the public.'

'I agree, Holmes, I have often been aware of the rather condescending manner adopted by the official police towards you. Yet without your help many a criminal would still be free to conduct his wicked activities.'

'Of course I do not include Lestrade and Shershey and one or two others. They do acknowledge my help; even if, sometimes, reluctantly. And, of course, I must include Inspector Nokes. Another thing, when we were examining the body of the victim I asked you to consider the size of the wound in the temple.'

'Yes, the police surgeon agreed with me that it was smaller than one would have expected from a revolver of the calibre found in the victim's hand.'

'My dear friend, we do have some important facts before us. Firstly, the professor was found still seated in his chair which means had he fired the gun himself then it would have dropped from his hand. It did not because it was placed there by the murderer. Therefore, it was not fired. Secondly, the assailant must have used a different gun; possibly an air-gun. They are often used by rifle clubs and therefore readily available. Many of them have a muzzle velocity equal to that imparted by exploding powder; hence the passage of the bullet completely through the skull and onward to be buried somewhere in the wall.'

'Well, that appears to have settled the method used by the murderer but not why. There has to be a motive, surely?'

'We cannot determine the motive until we have definitely established the identity of the assassin. This sets a problem because the professor did not, according to those close to him, appear to have any enemies. He was liked and admired. The motive, Watson, is more than likely to be found in the last page of the letter found in the professor's room. All I can do is to stretch my imagination and conclude that the professor, over a long period, gradually became aware the research conducted by the senior tutor was a plagiarism.'

'You mean Doctor Aspinoll.'

'Yes. I discovered from reading through the professor's diary that he had undertaken considerable research into the same subject as that of the tutor's original doctoral thesis. In doing so he had come to realise that much of it had been borrowed, though that may be too kind a word, from the work of another. He delayed telling the Dean in the hope that he was wrong or the culprit might confess. Eventually he decided that the good name of the college and of the university had to outweigh any other considerations. He may have confronted him with the evidence but to no avail. On the evening of the crime, I imagine, Aspinoll went to the professor's room to either plead with him or threaten him. I suggest the latter because this is a

177

premeditated crime. He was desperate. The thought of losing the McClusky stipend and the prodigious chair for which he was the preferred candidate, drove all other considerations out of his mind. He realised he had to kill the professor. He arrived armed with an air gun, and a revolver. He knew exactly what he intended to do.'

'I must confess, Holmes that is a masterly reconstruction of what you say happened. However, I must qualify that by saying that you postulate what might have happened not what did happen. Surely, there is insufficient evidence to point toward Aspinoll? Evidence which is of sufficient quality to convince a jury.'

'I agree. I have to establish his guilt so that there can be no reasonable doubt in the minds of a jury.'

'And the next step is?'

'The university gun club and a study of its list of members.'

The list revealed that of the total membership three were from St Edmunds. Aspinoll was one of the three.

On our way back from the gun club we discussed the significance of the suspect's membership.

'Surely, Holmes, there can be no doubt as to his guilt?'

'My dear friend, put your self in the place of a juryman. The defence council will emphasise that there is insufficient proof that Aspinoll is the guilty one of the three members of the gun club. Remember, the statements taken by Nokes provide no positive alibi for that night for any of the three.'

'Yes, but what of the evidence you have gathered concerning the plagiarism. Surely, that implicates Aspinoll without any doubt?'

'Perhaps, it could. However, I would not place too much reliance on it when submitted to a jury. They may not fully understand what it is all about. No, what I need to do is find the bullet and when I have it I can find the actual gun. Recall that when we were at the gun club we saw that many different types of air gun were being used. Each member has his own preference.'

Holmes and I returned to the professor's room with Inspector Nokes.

'Inspector, please will you sit in the chair and adopt, to the best of your memory, the attitude of the body as it was when you entered the room,' said Holmes. The inspector did as requested.

'Thank you. Ah, let me think. Yes, of course, perhaps you should hold your head up.'

The inspector was eventually seated to the satisfaction of Holmes.

'Now if I stretch a cord from your temple toward the wall I reach this point.' Holmes held the end of the string against the elaborately carved frame of a mirror.

'Let us take this down,' he said.

He examined the mirror and after a minute he pointed. 'Look here it is.' Using his penknife, Holmes extracted a lead ball.

'This, I am certain, came from an old air rifle of the Girandoni type favoured at one time by the Austrian army. Observe it is a ball and not the same as the bullet used in modern air-guns.'

'Dare I say, conclusive, Holmes?' I commented.

'Unfortunately you cannot. The list of gun club members, indeed, showed that many different types of gun were in use but none was a Girandoni. Inspector, we have to bring Aspinoll and a Girandoni together before we can proceed any further. Do you not agree?'

'I accept your advice, Mr Holmes. By the way, is a Girandoni a small gun?'

'Fortunately for our quest it is a somewhat clumsy weapon and therefore difficult to conceal. In the meantime I will have to give some thought to that particular problem. Perhaps we can meet here again tomorrow morning, say at ten.'

'Ten of the morrow then Mr Holmes.'

Once again we met in the professor's room. Holmes had asked the professor's servant to be with us as he had some questions to put to him.

'Can you recall if, on that dreadful night, Dr Aspinoll was carrying anything when he called on the professor? You did say you had seen him going up?'

'Yes, Sir,' replied the servant, 'I saw him and I am sure he was carrying his viola case.'

'Why would he take a viola case up to the professor?' asked Holmes.

'Oh, they were both fond of music and I understand that the professor gave the Doctor advice. They both played in the college amateur orchestra.'

'That means the professor's hand preference would be obvious to anyone who discussed and played music with him,' I interjected.

'A good point, Watson,' said Holmes 'unless, as you said before, someone is deliberately trying to confuse us.'

Holmes then put another question to the servant. 'How long was Dr Aspinoll with the professor and did you hear a viola being played?'

'I'm sorry, Sir, but I can't really say. I was with the other servants having supper.'

'So you did not hear a gun being fired between nine and ten?'

'No, Sir.'

'You have been most helpful. You may go; that is unless the Inspector has some questions.'

'None, thank you, Mr Holmes.'

When the servant had left the inspector said, 'Mr Holmes, the viola case, do you think it was used to carry the gun up to this room?'

'A possibility, yes. Mind you, a Girandoni, as I mentioned, is a rather clumsy weapon. However if he had left off the magazine I think you could get one in a viola case.'

'Obviously, we now have to find the gun,' said the inspector.

I commented, 'Cambridge town and the university together must provide thousands of hiding places. And, of course there is the Cam which, as with most rivers flowing through a town, provides a repository for unwanted items and, possibly, in this case, a gun. So, where do we start to look?'

'We don't, Watson. We let our suspect lead us to it. I say this because when I questioned him the other day I could see he was someone who treasured possessions of all types. His room was a virtual museum. Owning a working Girandoni could be extremely satisfying to him and I cannot see him throwing it away. I also determined, from his manner, that he had an inflated opinion of himself. His comments about other academics were of the most disdainful type. Also, I was sure he considered I was an incompetent amateur detective.'

'Do you not agree, Inspector?'

'Yes, I do Mr Holmes. Oh, of course, not his amateur remark. I too found his manner overbearing. So you think he still has the gun hidden away somewhere?'

'Certainly,' Holmes replied.

What I came to say next was done with some reluctance because I found my reasoning rather weak. Nevertheless, I pressed on. 'You know, Holmes, I cannot help going over the question of the sound of the gun being fired. It was heard but you conclude that it was not fired.'

'My dear friend, I confess I am going to test a theory on you before I state all the facts. You recall I often proceed this way when I value your opinion on a particular matter. It gives me a yardstick against which to measure it. If I were to divulge something to you too soon I am sure you will agree that your judgement might be influenced. Yes, a gun was fired but not the one found in the victim's hand. I am convinced the murderer paid a second visit to the lobby and there he fired another gun. This provided him with an alibi. If, as I believe, it was Aspinoll then he can claim that soon after the shot was heard he was with those who gathered at the foot of the stairs.'

'I confess, Mr Holmes, the sound of the shot and the time it occurred presented a puzzle when we come to consider Aspinoll might be the murderer. As my notes indicate, at least three people were near him at the time.'

'Inspector, did you examine the lobby when you made your first study of the murder scene?'

'I saw no reason to, Mr Holmes.'

'I suggest that is what we must now do.'

'What must we look for?'

'Any signs of a gun having been fired. He may have used a blank or he fired so as to hide the bullet. Although this is a premeditated crime I doubt he thought about using a blank round. It could be one detail out of many which eluded him.'

'If he fired into the wall it will be easy to find.'

Once we had made our way from the study into the lobby Holmes said, 'Facing us, Inspector, is this massive bookcase with some fat tomes. Let us examine them closely.'

Holmes using his magnifying glass moved slowly along each of the two middle rows.

'Ah, as I suspected. Look through my glass, Inspector, at these two volumes. You should be able to see clearly the scorching of the covers. A gun has been pushed between them and fired. I reason not only was the intention to disguise the fact a third gun was involved but also to deaden the sound so as to make it difficult for anyone to be certain if they heard it and if they did from where it had come.'

'Well, then he could have used a blank,' I suggested.

'I agree, Watson, but it makes no difference. Bullet or no bullet it is the sound of the gun and the time it was heard which are important.'

'Mr Holmes, I can satisfy the superintendent that enough evidence has been gathered to justify charging Dr Aspinoll with murder. He will be arrested.'

'I admire your confidence, Inspector. However, a word of caution. We have yet to find the gun and connect it, without any doubt, to the crime. Nevertheless, I realise you have got to make some progress and charging the doctor is all you can do for the time being. May I propose that you obtain a warrant to search Aspinoll's house. I understand he maintains a bachelor establishment about a mile or so down stream from here. You told us that when he let you examine his room here in the college he appeared confident that you would have found nothing of a suspicious nature.'

'There was nothing untoward. Yes, I agree his house must be searched. You and Dr Watson will come with me I trust?'

'Certainly, Inspector.'

The senior tutor's house, or I should say villa, was of the modern, rather pretentious style favoured by stockbrokers and gentlemen of the turf. It was not to my taste. However, we arrived at the front door armed with a warrant to search, and not to admire the villa's architecture. The door was opened by the housekeeper. She expressed surprise when told that Dr Aspinoll was in custody.

Our inspection of the various rooms failed to disclose what we were seeking. We were on the point of leaving when Holmes suggested, 'Inspector, let us make another scrutiny of the study.'

Once inside Holmes went immediately to the far end of the room and stood scanning the rows of books resting on rows of shelves. They extended from floor to ceiling. We waited to see what he would do next. He turned and began to pace the length of the room from the book shelves to the window at the front of the house. 'Fifteen paces, gentlemen. Now please follow me.'

He led us into the hallway and starting at the front door began pacing toward the green baize door that led to the servants' quarters. 'I make that thirty five paces. Please make a note, Watson. Now let us go into the music room.'

The music room was through a door on the right at the end of the hallway. Once inside Holmes paced the distance from the front to the back. 'I make that fifteen.'

Holmes led us back to the study and went up to the bookshelves. 'It's too dark in here please will you light that candle, Inspector.' Holding the candle close to the books Holmes moved it from side to side. At one point he stopped. 'Observe the flame.' We could clearly see it was being affected by a draught.

'Those distances you have noted down, Watson, show that if we add the fifteen paces of this room to the fifteen in the music room, thus making thirty, which leaves five needed to make the total of thirty five which is the distance from the front door to the end of the hallway. Five paces are missing and they have to be found behind these books.'

We set about taking down the books. 'We need only concern ourselves with those on the shelves which are within easy reach,' said Holmes.

Our efforts were rewarded when a catch normally hidden by the books was revealed and a section of the shelves could be pushed open to form a doorway leading to a hidden room. Inside, even by the feeble light of one candle, we could see many different objects. 'We've been looking for this vase for the past two years' exclaimed the inspector, 'and look at this, it's the Van Dyke stolen from Kings last year.'

We had come across the hoard of a kleptomaniac. Further searching disclosed the gun we were looking for. 'We now have the gun to match the bullet, which should be sufficient evidence to convict,' said Holmes.

Eventually, Aspinoll was tried, and paid the ultimate penalty.

On our way back to London I had posed to Holmes what I considered to be the important question of how Aspinoll was able to move the chest and then escape from the room.

'My reconstruction of the events was based on the rope fibres I detected when I was examining the floor. I could make out traces of fibre and the mark of a rope round the feet of the chest. It was clear to me that a rope had been used to pull the chest into position to bar the door after the murderer had left the room. I observed that there was a sufficient gap below the bottom of the door to allow a rope to be passed through.'

'I must again apologise for my failure to grasp all the complications of the affair, but you did not find any rope tied to the legs of the chest.'

'Simple, my dear Watson, he used a rope twice as long as was necessary, one that stretched round the legs of the chest. Once he had hauled the chest into position by pulling on both ends he pulled on one end and recovered the rope.'

'Holmes, you asked me if I remembered where the linen basket was. Why?'

'Because the rope used to move the chest could have been hidden under the dirty linen. The murderer could have placed it there some hours before he needed to use it. As we have said, the Girandoni is an air rifle and therefore does not make a loud noise when fired. Therefore Aspinoll killed the professor without anyone hearing the shot. After he had committed his dreadful act he took the rope from the basket without any one seeing him. He then arranged the rope round the legs of the chest and moved it so as to block the door. He then put the rope back under the linen intending to recover it at a later time. It was at this point he returned to the lobby to fire the pistol

187

which alerted the witnesses, which was why Aspinoll arrived first on the scene for them all to be confronted by the barred door. Although such a reconstruction has to consider the possibility that he might have been seen. However, I suppose he took the chance and won. He had the advantage of working in the lobby and therefore out of sight. We have to remember that the professor's rooms are the only ones at the top of the stairs. Therefore it was likely that, other than his servant, he would not have had many visitors at that time of the night.'

Once again my friend's observations, reasoning and conclusions led to the solving of a crime.

THE END

THE WHISTLES THAT DID NOT SOUND

In which Sherlock Holmes and Dr Watson have to find the location of stolen money and apprehend thieves. At considerable risk, Holmes seizes the stolen goods from under the noses of the villains.

My great friend, the foremost detective in the kingdom, was reluctant to stay away from the Great Wen. One night at the most was his preference. Occasionally the circumstances of a case demanded a sojourn of more than one night away. Thus we were staying in one of the two large station hotels in the City of Birmingham. I will not burden the reader with which of the two because of an incident that occurred.

On the morning of our last day away from Baker Street we were having breakfast. Holmes was applying butter to a piece of toast and said, 'pass the marmalade please.'

I replied. 'There is none.'

'What no marmalade!' He beckoned a waiter. 'Please bring some marmalade, there is none on this table.'

'We do not have any marmalade, Sir. Can I bring you some jam?'

'Jam, jam on my toast! What an absurd idea. We are British not French.'

Holmes dismissed the waiter. When the headwaiter presented our bills Holmes exclaimed, 'four shillings and sixpence for bed and breakfast. Outrageous. Even more outrageous is the absence of marmalade. I will complain to the management.'

Leaving aside the incident with the marmalade, the reason we were in Birmingham was a daring raid on a bank in one of the affluent suburbs of the city. The manager of the bank and his wife and child had been kidnapped. Under duress he had had to divulge the numbers of the combination lock on the bank vault. The thieves broke through the wall from the adjacent premises, opened the vault and made off with bank notes, sovereigns and valuables from the deposit boxes. Holmes was asked to help the Birmingham police track down the criminals and recover the money and the valuables before the villains had time to dispose of them. Time, therefore, was important. We accompanied police inspector Campion of the Birmingham City Police to question the bank manager.

'Although you have had a dreadful experience, Mr James,' said Holmes 'I should like to ask you some questions, but if you feel it is too soon after your ordeal please say so. I shall understand.'

'No, I will be all right, Mr Holmes. The sooner you are able to locate the villains and recover the bank's money the better.'

'Although you have given the police an account of what happened I should prefer to hear it from your own lips. Pray start at the moment when you and your family were kidnapped. I understand you were on your way for a holiday by the sea at Llandudno and that you had left your chief accountant in charge.'

'Yes, we were going to be away for two weeks.'

'You were attacked outside the station by a number of men.'

'Yes, that is what happened. The villains set upon us as I was helping my wife and daughter to alight from a cab. At gun point I was thrust into another cab. At the time I did not know what was happening to my wife and daughter. A blanket was thrown over my head and the cab set off at a smart pace.'

'So you became separated from your family.'

'That was the most dreadful part of the whole affair.'

'Did you attempt to resist being bundled into the cab?'

'I struggled but one of them said, "Get in and keep quiet or you'll not see your wife and daughter again". What else could I do?'

'Did you get any indication of where you were being taken?'

'They kept the blanket over my head. We must have been going for about two or three hours before the cab stopped and I was bustled into a large house.'

'Did you hear any distinctive sounds during the journey? Did you hear the noises of a large town or city?'

'I regret, Mr Holmes that I was so concerned for the fate of my wife and daughter that I failed to notice any particular sounds. I'm sorry. I am not being of much help.'

'Don't be. I quite understand. What type of house was it?'

'A large villa. I was taken up to a room at the top. To my surprise they produced a postcard having a view of Llandudno and made me write to my parents saying how we were enjoying our two weeks holiday. They said that if I did not write then my wife and daughter would suffer. Obviously I had to write the card'

'Did they get the card?'

'Yes, and that's why at first they were not concerned.'

'A clever move on the villains' part. I expect they posted it inside a letter to an accomplice in Llandudno who then re-posted it with the correct postmark.'

'Were the windows covered to prevent you seeing where you were?'

'Other than curtains, they were not covered.'

'What could you see? A hill, houses, perhaps, a tall building or chimney?'

'Not much. My view was limited to the edge of a copse.'

'Which direction were you looking, north, south…?'

'Definitely east because in the morning the sun rose up behind the trees.'

'Good, that may be important. Now, as we know, your bank was broken into and the vault door opened using the correct numbers for the combination lock. No doubt you were forced to divulge them.'

'Mr Holmes I did my best to resist their threats of physical violence. Do you know, they even left an illustrated book of medieval tortures in the room?'

'Did they torture you then?'

'No but I had to give way in the end to something I suppose is worse than torture.'

'Oh, and what was that?'

'When I continued to refuse to give them the combination numbers one of them produced a small box from his pocket saying, "I think this will change your mind." He opened the box and what I saw filled me with horror and at the same time the desire to leap on my tormenter.'

'Go on.'

'It was one of my dear wife's fingers.'

'How could you have been sure?'

'Because there, staring me in the face, was her wedding ring and the diamond keeper ring. They said that for each day I refused their demands there would be another of her fingers.'

'You were faced with a terrible choice. I can well understand why you had to give them the numbers.'

'Now tell me what happened after you gave them the combination.'

'I heard some shouting and laughing below and then I heard a carriage drive off.'

'Another thing, Mr James, would you recognise the men who took you and were in the house?'

'Perhaps I might recognize those who seized us outside the station but the others who were in the house wore masks when ever they came to the room.'

I listened to this account and the questions with great interest. Holmes next said to the bank manager, 'Mr James, let us return to the now important matter of locating the robbers' lair in which you were held. Did you hear anything that made you think they had brought the stolen money back to the house?'

'I am certain they did, Mr Holmes. The last night I was there I heard them moving back and forth in the hallway and later there was much shouting and drunken singing. That is when they must have returned from the bank and they were celebrating.'

'We must try and find where the house is so that the police can apprehend them and recover the money. As you could not see much from your window we have to rely on what you could hear. Are you certain that the house was not in a town?'

'Even during the day all I could hear were the usual sounds of the countryside. I felt very isolated. They even, for some reason, took away my watch. I had to tell the time from the position of the sun. At night I lay awake worrying about my family and listening to the distant sounds of trains.'

'Trains, you say. Were they close?'

'I thought at the time they were about a mile away.'

Holmes said nothing for a minute. He was obviously thinking about the sounds of the trains. So was I. When he spoke I was not surprised when he said, 'Watson, remember the Tiptree affair and how your interest in railways provided some important clues. Please, will you try and put questions to Mr James from which we can locate the railway. It could be an important clue as to where the house is.'

'Mr James could you hear many trains,' I asked.

'Well, now you ask, Dr Watson, I remember I could hear many. I was surprised at the number. Even at night the line was busy.'

'My next question is, were they travelling fast?'

'Some did not make much noise, but others made noises that suggested that not only were they moving slowly but that they were struggling up a hill.'

'Mr James you are being most helpful. We now have a busy stretch of line, which, I surmise, had a steep gradient. You were hearing trains moving down the hill and others struggling upward. Could you say that, in your experience of travelling by train that their whistles were distinctive?'

'Well, come to think of it, Doctor, I was surprised at the amount of whistling that took place. Although I cannot say I could tell one whistle from another.'

'Were they just the usual types of whistling?'

'I'm not sure what the usual type is, but I can tell you that the engines sounded as if they were talking to each other.'

'That is an interesting observation, I must say.'

'In some ways, Doctor, those sounds, particularly the whistling, kept me in touch with the world outside my prison. One night there were no sounds and I felt lost.'

'No sounds at all. Surprising. Did you hear trains moving again in the morning?'

'There was the sound of a train now and then moving back and forth. I did not hear the usual noise of trains passing at frequent short intervals.'

'What day was that Mr James,' asked Holmes.

'That was on the Tuesday.'

'And the next day you were released.'

'Yes. I was put in a cab with a blanket over my head and driven for some time. Eventually I was pushed out of the cab and I found myself close to my own house. To my intense relief my wife and daughter were there. They too had been held captive but they had no idea where they had been held.'

'Had they come to any harm?'

'Fortunately not. Apart from being subjected to severe anxiety about my fate, they had been well treated.'

'As I suspect, none of your wife's fingers had been cut off. Am I right?'

'Yes, Mr Holmes. They played a cruel deception to make me give up the numbers. But whose finger was it?'

'Perhaps they stole it from a mortuary or a hospital.'

'Not a pleasant thought, Mr Holmes.'

'I agree. The more important thing is that you and your family are now safe. I consider it best that we stop at this point,' said Holmes. 'You have given us much to think about. Thank you so much for remembering some important details. '

Holmes, Inspector Campion and I adjourned to the inspector's office to consider what Mr James had been able to remember.

'This is your chance, Watson, to exercise your interest in railways for the benefit of the case'

'Two facts stand out. One, the engines talking to each other, as Mr James put it, and, two, no trains were running on the Tuesday. Often when more than one engine whistles, their drivers are exchanging information. At the foot of an incline, for example, if a train had a second engine to provide extra push, the driver at the head of the train would indicate that he was about to start by an agreed whistle code. I know of two places where this happens. Between Exeter St Davids and Queen Street stations and on the Lickey Incline which is not far from here on the line to Bristol. I am sure there may be others. He mentioned that he could hear engines struggling, as he put it, to climb a gradient.'

'Well done, Watson.' said Holmes 'I consider that the most significant recollection of Mr James is that there were no trains to be heard on the Monday night. Inspector, assuming it is the Lickey Incline then I suggest the stationmaster at New Street will be able to tell us if, on Tuesday on the Bristol line, there were no trains running on that day.'

'I see what you are getting at, Mr Holmes. However, Mr James told us that his cab journey seemed to take two or three hours. But it would not take that long to get there.'

'Not necessarily so, Inspector. In a number of cases with which I have been involved, cunning criminals have taken people for seemingly long rides by deliberately going round, as it were, in circles to confuse them over how far they had travelled.'

Having determined, by telegraph, from the New Street stationmaster, that on the Monday evening the Midland main line between Bristol and Birmingham had been blocked by the wreckage of a train of wagons at Bromsgrove, we spread a railway map on the table.

'This map of yours, Inspector,' said Holmes, 'provides us with Bromsgrove station as the starting point for our search. Let us see. If we describe a circle of, say, a ten mile radius, discard the area enclosed to the east of the railway, and take into account the position of the Lickey Incline we are left with a segment within which, if Mr James' recollections are correct, sits the villa. I propose we go straight away to Bromsgrove station.'

We took a train from New Street station and on the way we went over what we had learned from the bank manager.

'Inspector, you say the thieves broke into the bank from the adjoining premises?' asked Holmes.

'Yes, they were most determined.'

'I anticipate that you are about to tell me that those premises were unoccupied.'

'Well, yes they were. How did you know?

'From experience, Inspector. Nothing more. Just experience'

The inspector continued his account of the robbery. 'The premises consisted of a shop with domestic rooms above. About two weeks before there had been a fire and work was underway to make good the damage. Workmen were seen going in and out and no one thought that unusual. They broke through the party wall on Monday night. That was after they had forced the combination numbers from the manager. They were cunning because they did not immediately go off with the stolen goods but waited until one hour before the bank opened. No one questioned why a wagon outside was being loaded with building material and sacks. Obviously they had put the money and the valuables in the sacks.'

'Inspector, this type of attack on a building holding valuables is becoming too common. I had intended to write a small book on the subject of defending property and how to anticipate criminal activity by dedicated observation at all times. It will also remind readers that the carpenter, the bricklayer and other types of workmen can move in and out of premises without being questioned. Their garb and tools are a passport.'

'I have encouraged my friend to write such a book,' said I.

'I am sure it could be of great value to everyone, including the police. I trust you will continue with it Mr Holmes,' said the inspector.

'I thought long about it but have reached the conclusion that any benefit to readers wishing to protect their property and goods would be outweighed by the information it would provide criminals. They would absorb, I am certain, every detail and take pains to ensure that their actions circumvented my advice,' replied Holmes.

The driver of the cab we hired at Bromsgrove must have been somewhat puzzled by the erratic orders given by his passengers. Up one lane, down another, go back. Stop. For two hours we scoured the lanes and stopped to examine isolated houses until at last we came upon a villa in a location which matched the bank manager's description. Leaving the cab we made our way carefully round the outside of the house. We used the trees and bushes to hide our movements. We were able to verify that there were upper windows facing east. Importantly, we could hear clearly the sounds of trains a few miles away assaulting the Lickey Incline with much whistling.

'This is the place, I am sure, Inspector.'

'We are dealing with some desperate villains. According to Mr James there were at least three men in the house. I do not have a gun. I'll take the cab back to the police station in the town we passed about four miles down this road and gather some constables.'

'Yes, do that,' said Holmes. 'In the meantime we will watch the house. Have you your service revolver with you Watson?' I showed it.

We had only been waiting for about a quarter of an hour when we saw a horse being harnessed to a four-wheeler standing in front of the house. The cab was being loaded with sacks.

'They are going to escape with the money. We must stop them,' exclaimed Holmes.

'How?' was my response as I realised that once again Holmes was leading me into danger.

'What I am going to try and do is work my way through the bushes until I am close to the cab. You stay here and have your gun ready in the event I run into trouble.'

Those who had loaded the sacks went back into the house. Then one came out and started toward the carriage. A voice called out from within the house. 'Get to the Bull. They'll be waiting for you.' This prompted him to turn and go back into the house and we could hear him protesting about something.

'Now's my chance, Watson. They are all in the house,' said Holmes quietly.

'Take care or they'll catch you.' Before I could say another word Holmes leaped onto the box and whipped up the horse. The carriage moved off and gathered speed just as two of the villains rushed out of the house and gave chase. They failed to stop Holmes and the last I saw of him was urging the horse into a gallop. I crept out of sight into the bushes and awaited events, expecting any minute to be discovered and having to defend myself with one revolver against possibly two or three desperate armed criminals. From inside the house came much shouting and foul language. I assumed one of the thieves was being berated by the others for losing the carriage and its valuable contents.

After an anxious half hour the carriage returned accompanied by another containing the inspector and four constables. I learned later that Holmes had met them half way to the police station.

The house was found to contain three robbers and the valuables taken from the deposit boxes. The bank notes and bags of sovereigns were in the vehicle 'kidnapped' by Holmes.

We journeyed back to London by a North Western express. Holmes wiled away the two hours by commenting on some of the lonely farmhouses we passed. 'You know, Watson, when I see these isolated dwellings set in the clear air of the countryside far from the bustling cities and their sulphurous atmospheres and above all criminal activity, I remind myself that their apparent idyllic situation can harbour deeds of the most violent nature.'

THE END

THE TARRANT VALLEY ALIBI

In which a hoard of Saxon gold artefacts worth many thousands of pounds is discovered in a lane following a landslip. Some of it is then stolen and Sherlock Holmes is able to examine the suspect's alibi and deduce where he had hidden the treasure.

On a mild October day the principal room in 221B Baker Street exhibited its customary after-breakfast disorder. Newspapers were scattered on the floor around Holmes' favourite chair and the atmosphere was mostly of tobacco smoke.

I ventured to interrupt my friend's concentration on his paper, 'I say, Holmes, did you read about the theft of the Saxon hoard down in Dorset. It had been moved from where it had been unearthed to the crypt of a nearby church. Apparently, antiquarians from the British Museum were down there studying and recording the different items of the treasure. It seems some villain entered the crypt, pointed a shot gun and ordered them to lie down while he scooped up some of the most valuable gold plates and cups and put them into a sack and left.'

'Yes, of course, the hoard was discovered when an attempt was made to clear a mass of earth caused by a landslip. A fierce gale had uprooted trees and disturbed the side of a sunken road. It also undermined the foundations of the covered bridge that joined the eastern half of Lord Rushton's park with the western deer park. The bridge collapsed and completely blocked the road. It stayed blocked while the parish disputed with Lord Rushton's steward over who was responsible for clearing away the debris. I read that the villagers of Tarrant Megville Parva, to the north of the blocked sunken road, were only able to reach the lower parts of the Tarrant Valley by travelling a long way round; either to the east or to the west. I also remember reading about the dispute over the ownership of the treasure.'

'Surely, Holmes, I would have thought this was a case of treasure trove that could eventually benefit those who came across the gold artefacts when they were clearing the road?'

'I doubt that it is as simple as that, Watson. As I see it, there are three parties involved. First there is the Crown, then the labourers who were clearing the debris of the landslip and, finally, Lord Rushton the owner of the estate through which the public highway passes. If I recall correctly, the Crown has first right to treasure trove. Those who discover it can claim the antiquarian market value and the British Museum houses the treasure. However, if someone can claim it by right of inheritance then it is theirs. Lord Rushton would have to provide a genealogical tree without any gaps going back for over a thousand years. Essentially, his claim can be based on the undoubted fact that the hoard had remained on his land for over a thousand years.'

'Was there any information about the villain who stole the cups and plates at gunpoint?'

'Yes, I remember reading that he had wound a scarf about his face. However, one of those present in the crypt happened to be a local man from the village who was helping the British Museum investigators. He was a cobbler and recognised the villain's built-up shoe used to correct a deformed foot. Joel Hedger, who has a clubfoot, has been apprehended. He claims that at the time of the robbery he was with friends at an inn ten miles to the south. A number of drinkers in the inn swear that he was there at the time. They particularly recall his presence because he helped them to put out a fire which had started in the wood shed at the back of the inn.'

Our discussion about the stolen artefacts was interrupted when Mrs Hudson entered and handed Holmes a telegram. I anticipated that a telegram at that time of the morning usually meant a new mystery for my friend to solve. I was not mistaken.

'Watson, my cousin Wellbos, the Chief Constable of Wessex, once again asks for help. And, not surprisingly, it is the very crime we are considering at this moment.'

'No doubt you will want me to consult Bradshaw and find the most convenient train to the Tarrant Valley.'

'If you would be so kind. Oh, this is interesting,' he waved a second telegram. 'This is from Mycroft. All it says is, "Your help will be appreciated."'

'No doubt the Tarrant Valley robbery,' said I.

The next morning we were met at Blandford station by Inspector Stubbs of the Wessex Constabulary. He had a carriage waiting and soon we were moving at a smart pace through the Dorset countryside. The leaves of the trees had achieved their greatest intensity of gold, yellow and red hues.

'As your telegram requested, Mr Holmes, we will first go to where the hoard was found and then onto the church.' said the inspector,

'Yes, thank you. Although I doubt I should find much of importance at the first, there may be something of interest to find at the church. Out of curiosity I should also like to see the damage to the road and the bridge.'

As we were about to enter one of the many rustic villages that were strung like beads along the valley of the Tarrant the inspector said, 'we are about to pass the house where the chief constable has arranged for you to stay with friends of his. There it is on the left, Uplea House.'

'I am indebted to my cousin. He has chosen a delightful spot.'

That remark by Holmes came as a surprise because he rarely commented on his surroundings and particularly on their beauty. A rustic idyll was of no greater import to him than the busy streets of London. For my part I welcomed the prospect of a bed in a family house instead of some musty hotel.

The winding lane that led north, from the Blandford to Salisbury road, eventually brought us to where the covered bridge had collapsed. On both sides there was a large heap of broken masonry and brickwork.

'The place where the treasure was found is a bit further on,' said Inspector Stubbs.

We saw how a great portion of the side of the sunken road had slid down. Although the debris had been moved to one side to allow us to proceed, a number of men were still digging in the hope that more treasure might be found.

The inspector pointed out where the treasure had been buried under the ground at the edge of Lord Rushton's park saying, 'It was with some ancient graves. The landslip moved it some ten or so yards out onto the road. '

'I've seen enough here, please let us move on to the church,' said Holmes.

A mile or two up the road we came to an ancient village and its church. The door to the crypt was unbolted and we went into low vaulted space. At first Holmes appeared to find nothing of particular interest. Then he said, 'let me examine the door and its fastening. You say, Inspector, that when the thief left he locked the museum people in so that they could not raise the alarm. And, of course, he chose a night when a strong gale kept most sensible people behind their doors.'

'That's so, Mr Holmes, it was an extremely wild night.'

When we were outside the door Holmes asked, 'Inspector, what did Hedger do to this lock?'

'He slipped a piece of wood through the bolt,' was the reply.

'Have you still got it?'

'Yes, here it is.'

He produced the length of wood that had jammed the bolt. Holmes studied it closely,

'This has been carefully whittled to make a good fit. Otherwise, he might have picked up any length of wood lying in the churchyard. This tells us that, as I am sure you will agree, the robbery was premeditated on the part of the villain,' said he.

'I agree he must have prepared it in anticipation of locking the door.'

'I understand, Inspector,' said Holmes, 'that the suspect has a deformed foot and that the local cobbler helping the antiquarians recognised the special boot he had made for him.'

'That is why I arrested him because such evidence points clearly to him.'

'Did your men find the gun?'

'So far they have not come across it.'

'Well, as it was not fired I do not think it is of importance and I doubt that we would find anything on it to prove it was the one used by the thief. Inspector, may I question the suspect and can Dr Watson be with us?

'Most certainly, Mr Holmes. The suspect is sticking to his story that he was with friends at the Navigation Inn ten miles from here at the time of the robbery. Shall we say ten forenoon at the police station in Blandford? A carriage will be at the door of Uplea House at nine.'

We stayed that night, as arranged, with the Bryanstones, a most delightful and appealing family. We had an interesting discussion about the robbery and who had claim to the gold artefacts. I recall that our host was more concerned over the propensity for the river Tarrant to overflow its banks; as it had done the day after the robbery. One could not avoid the aroma that is typical of the farmlands. As we went on to talk about trees and hedges and farming matters, Holmes appeared oblivious of his surroundings and spent the greater part of the time sitting with his fingers steepled and saying little. After a time he said, 'Mr Bryanstone, as you know, one of my interests is the study of criminal activity. As you are a Justice of the

Peace would you say that such activity is common out here in these bucolic surroundings?'

'In view of our discussion about the stealing of the Saxon gold I would like to emphasise that a crime involving property of such value is fairly rare around here.'

'What of gangs of criminals who might come from the Capital, for example, intent on an organised robbery of one of the noble houses I observed as we travelled here? I mention this because I have to consider the possibility that the suspect in the Saxon gold case may have been recruited by a gang from London. I have put that probability to inspector Stubbs.'

'I agree there is such a possibility, Mr Holmes. The suspect is well known to the bench. However, this must not go beyond these four walls, because we must avoid deliberately prejudicing any future jury.'

'We understand, don't we Watson.'

I nodded agreement and, as Holmes once again seemed completely absorbed in his own thoughts, I led the talk toward something I had observed when we were being shown round the splendid garden of Uplea House. 'Mr Bryanstone, I could not help but notice a group of destitute looking men seated on a bench outside the kitchen door. Oh,' I paused, 'I apologise, they could have been your outdoor servants.'

'No need, Doctor. They were unfortunately destitute. I have seen the dreadful slums of your city and the appalling conditions in which so many live. We do not have such slums out here, thank God, but all the same there is a lot of extreme poverty. Those men would have come to my wife for help. She provides them with ale, bread and cheese. It is heartbreaking to see them slipping a piece of cheese or a hunk of bread into a pocket for their family who more than likely are living under a hedge. There has been a great upheaval on the land and many farmhands, as well as their womenfolk, have lost their employment. Many farmers round here employ steam ploughing engines that take the place of both horses and men. I cannot see the end of this march of the machine that many call progress. In some ways you could say that the railway my father had built to take chalk from his quarry changed the social structure as horses and wagons and their drivers were no longer required.'

'You mean the Tarrant Valley Railway?'

'Yes, Dr Watson, over there on the wall is the original map of the survey of the line's path.'

I stood up and went over to the glass-framed survey map of the railway. I studied it for a few minutes and then I commented, 'I see it descends all the way down from the quarry to the river. Most interesting. It is, as you say, an example of machines that have and may change all our lives in the future. I understand you are a scientist and hold the chair of natural philosophy at one of the Oxford colleges. Is that your opinion?'

'That is so, Doctor,' he replied. 'I foresee many changes that science can bring about. Some may prove to be of benefit to mankind, whereas others may not. For example did you observe the apparatus that I have erected on the roof of this house?'

'You mean those black flat panels and all those pipes?'

'Yes. You see, I harness the heat of the sun's rays on the black surface of the metal that covers one half of the roof. That in turn heats the water flowing within each panel.'

'An amazing idea,' was my response. I refrained from displaying my limited acquaintance with things mechanical by asking what if there was no sunshine.

'May I also ask about the strange tingling sensation in my fingers when touching a doorknob?'

'Of course you may. It is part of a burglar alarm system for town houses using electricity, with which I have been experimenting.'

He introduced us to many other pieces of unfamiliar apparatus and objects. Our host was undoubtedly a true savant.

After supper that evening I said to our host, 'Mr Bryanstone you certainly have a most charming house and garden in an idyllic location. I envy you.'

'You might not, Doctor, if you had to live all your days here. I would not call it idyllic. As we were discussing earlier, life is rarely idyllic for farm workers and the lower orders in general.'

'Possibly not for them but for yourself, surely, this must be preferred to a life in a city?' I responded.

'Well there is the habit of the Tarrant inundating both the house and the garden, and the boundary disputes to settle with our neighbours. There are also the meetings of the Parish Council that I attend. You would find it hard to believe the petty arguments that arise over often the most trivial matter.

Nevertheless, I suppose I must admit it is a pleasant life for my family.'

'Presumably, the fallen bridge is adding to the council's troubles.'

'Yes, we are having trouble over it with Lord Rushton's steward.'

The next morning we went to the police station in Blandford where Holmes questioned the suspect. He was a thick set man of medium height and when he was brought into the room his club foot was evident.

'This gentleman is Mr Holmes from London. He is going to put some questions to you.'

'Never 'erd of 'im,' was the response.'

'Just answer the questions, Hedger' ordered the inspector.

Holmes looked steadily at the suspect, his gaze moving upward from his boots to his head. Then he said, 'Hedger, you claim that at the time of the robbery you were with friends at the Navigation Inn ten miles to the south of here. Is that correct?'

'That's right mister. They'll say that oi was with 'em. I b'aint be near the church. I knows they'll remember oi as being there because oi was playing ballinhol for the Navigation team that night.

'Ballinhol, you say.'

'That's right, Ow could oi been where the Inspector says I be at. I swears I was in the Navigation all the time.'

'Show me your hands,' said Holmes.

The suspect held out his hands and Holmes examined them, paying particular attention to the rough and broken nails.

'The jacket you've got on, is it the one you were wearing on the night you say you were in the Navigation?'

'Of course, oi've only got the one.'

'That will do Inspector. I have no more questions to put for the time being.'

When the suspect had been led back to his cell Holmes asked, 'Inspector, what of his claim that he was playing ballinhol at the inn with friends?'

'I questioned the innkeeper and he told me that on that night there had been a ballinhol match with the team from the Crown and Stag. It started soon after half past eight. He replied that he could not be absolutely certain that the suspect was there before the match started because there were three times the usual number of drinkers.'

'Did you question any of the men the suspect claimed he was drinking with?'

'They could not say definitely whether he had been with them for some time before the game started. One or two said that as he was always with them nearly most evenings then he must have been there; although he definitely helped to put out the fire in the wood shed.'

'Inspector, may we now go to the suspect's house.'

'Of course. It's not far from here, Mr Holmes.'

After visiting the suspect's house we went back to Uplea House where Holmes summed up some aspects of the case.

'When we consider some of the facts, among the more important is that the thief entered the crypt as the church clock struck eight times. Was that by chance or by intention? Of importance also is the difference in time between the robbery and ballinhol game in the inn ten miles to the south. The alibi placed the villain in the inn at half past that hour. Therefore, how could he have travelled the ten miles in half an hour? The alternative routes to avoid the blocked road are each at least fifteen miles in length. Even with a strong and swift horse, the storm and the poor conditions of the roads meant that it would have needed about an hour to complete the ride. The weight of the stolen artefacts and having a clubfoot would have added to a rider's difficulties on such a night.'

The next morning at breakfast in Uplea House we became aware of a most appetising aroma coming from the kitchen.

'Blackberry and apple pie I wager,' I remarked.

Holmes remained absorbed in a newspaper and expressed his agreement of my conjecture with just a grunt. Some minutes later he dashed down the paper and exclaimed, 'did you say blackberry?'

'Yes, blackberry and apple pie.'

'Watson, you have given me an idea.'

'What is that, old chap?'

'Well you recall that when the inspector took us to the suspect's house there was a farm labourer's cream-coloured smock hanging in the hallway.'

'That's a common garment in this part of the country.'

'Indeed it is. Its importance to our investigation is the dark purple staining on the smock which might be blackberry juice.'

'Again, I fail to see any connection between the suspect and the crime because of some stains on his smock.'

'On their own, perhaps, the stains are of little or no importance. However, when I was permitted to examine the suspect's hands for evidence, under the fingernails for example, I could not help but observe the great number of scratches. Furthermore, even you observed the large scratch that had become septic on the suspect's face. You must have gone blackberrying when you were a boy Watson. It could often be a painful occupation, particularly if one reached too far into a bush.'

'Yes, of course. So our suspect went blackberrying. I must say a rather innocent pursuit.'

'Not so innocent, I suggest. It could be that the stolen gold artefacts have been hidden in one of the many large blackberry bushes that abound around here.'

'Indeed, Holmes, I noticed that there are many and some are, as you say, large. To search all will take some time. Time in which an accomplice of the suspect can recover them and take them away from Dorset.'

'I am now not inclined to believe that Hedger has an accomplice. I am sure that within a day or two of being told that the treasure was being kept in the church crypt he decided to act on his own; prepare the piece of wood to jam the door bolt, pick up his shotgun, realise that the storm would hide his purpose and act without further delay. If, as I am now convinced, he was acting on his own he made the mistake, that many a thief has done, of failing to consider what to do with the loot. He heard or read about the many gold cups and plates and ornaments and, without thinking further, said to himself, "I must have them." Only when he found himself with a sack full of gold did he realise he did not know what to do next. His only course was to hide it until he was able to dispose of the contents in exchange for money.'

'All we have to go on, Holmes, is your conjecture about the blackberry bushes. Which means that somewhere along the thief's route there has to be a large bush. Perhaps more than one.'

'Yes, that is a problem. However, we can simplify our search by deducing the route taken on the night of the robbery. As we have learned, the direct route was barred by the landslip and the fallen bridge so the villain had to go round by over fifteen miles either to the east or to the west. As we agreed, such a journey on a wild and stormy night on horse back and with a disability would have taken longer than thirty minutes.'

'Well if we discount the use of a carriage of some kind on such a night, we are left with the question of which route and which conveyance. A balloon? Certainly not in a southwest gale. So how?'

'Indeed, so how,' replied Holmes.

At that moment, carried on the wind, was the sound of a shrill whistle.

'I know you consider my acquired interest in railways rather peculiar, except when I can assist with one of your investigations, but that whistle reminds me that we are close to the Tarrant Valley Railway. I was discussing it with our host whose father built it and the chalk quarry it serves. '

'Were you? Never heard of it. Why did you not arrange that we travel down here by it instead of on the South Western, and that long wait at Templecombe for the Somerset and Dorset train to Blandford?'

'It is a mineral line running the length of the Tarrant valley. It conveys chalk from the head of the valley to a wharf on the Stour. I believe the chalk is of a particular kind that is much in demand.'

'Watson, your interest in railways could be useful at this point in our investigation. Could the thief have travelled on a train that night?'

'I doubt that any trains run at night. All the same I am sure a visit to the top of the line might be useful to us. I have observed, from the survey map of the line our host showed me, that the railway starts in the chalk quarry located only a few hundred yards from the church. It also ends close to the inn where the suspect claimed he was drinking with friends.'

We continued with our breakfast and were joined by our host. 'This marmalade, Mr Bryanstone, is magnificent,' Holmes said, 'I take a great interest in this type of preserve. Where does it come from?'

'No further, Mr Holmes, than from our kitchen. My wife supervises cook in the making of our own marmalade. She also takes delight in winning a prize at the local parish summer fete with her rock cakes. I am certain she would be delighted to let you have a jar to take back to London.'

'I should be most grateful.'

At our next meeting with the inspector Holmes said, 'I should like to visit the quarry and its railway please.' Accompanied by the inspector, we went to the quarry. In the sidings were trains of small wagons being loaded with chalk. A small locomotive set off at the head of a train on its way to the river Stour. Holmes surveyed the scene and then asked the foreman, a Mr White, who was conducting us around the scene of activity, 'am I correct in observing that a single wagon can be pushed along by one of the quarrymen without too much difficulty.'

'That's so Mr Holmes.'

'Mr White, you are aware, no doubt, that the Inspector has detained someone on suspicion of stealing some of the Saxon treasure.'

'I am aware and I know the suspect well, Mr Holmes, because at one time Hedger worked here. He often gave me trouble and he's been up before the bench a few times.'

'Thank you for that particular piece of information. You are being most helpful'

I commented, 'Mr White, I was studying a map of the railway yesterday. I see that the engine is always at the same end of a train. Is that because a train of wagons might break away and run down the gradients between here and the end of the line if the engine were not there to hold them back?

'You are right, Dr Watson, although each wagon has a simple pole brake, a man could not apply enough effort to stop a runaway train. The engine leads down toward the Stour and in the other direction pushes the empty wagons back to here.'

'Do the engines remain here at night?' asked Holmes.

'No, there is an engine shed near the wharf on the Stour. Each morning they push back all the empty wagons,' replied the foreman.

'Mr White, are the downward gradients significantly steep?' asked Holmes.

'Moderately so. It is downhill all the way except for a short length in the middle. Remember we are over six hundred feet above sea level at this point.'

'So if someone were to steal a wagon they would rely on the speed gained to carry them across the level stretch.

'That is right, Mr Holmes. They could,' he replied.

Turning to the inspector Holmes said, 'I am certain that the thief used one of the wagons to escape at a speed. I assume, faster than that of a galloping horse. Would it be possible to arrange with Mr White for an inspection of the blackberry bushes that grow close to the railway?''

'Mr Holmes, you think the stolen goods are hidden in a blackberry bush?'

'I do indeed. And not too far in. There is a strong possibility that our suspect stopped at some point on his way down to the end of the line to hide a sack containing the artefacts he had snatched from the crypt. I suggest you pay particular attention to those bushes that lie close to where the line levels off.'

On our return to Uplea House I did not immediately question Holmes' conclusion about the probable location of the blackberry bush hiding the stolen artefacts. I was trying to reason in my mind why he had arrived at it. Only when we reached the house did I raise the subject

'Holmes, you gave most precise advice concerning the most probable bush to look under.'

'Come, come, Watson, picture in your mind the villain pushing one of the wagons to the start of the descent. He lets it gather speed. He is intent on hiding the sack but where? He then realises that one of the blackberry bushes that grew in profusion alongside the line could serve as a cache. He sees a suitable one close to where the line is level. The wagon begins to slow down and he applies the brake and it stops. He hides the sack and then is able to push the wagon a short distance to the start of the next downward stretch.'

'A most interesting reconstruction Holmes. I see how he was able to reach the inn within half an hour. Although those at the inn could not say with certainty that he was with them before the ballinhol match started, he definitely helped to put out the fire in the wood shed which he must have started, to make sure he was noticed. Your observation of the scratches on the hands and face and the blackberry stains on the smock are vital clues. And, of course, the fact that he has been employed at the quarry at one time indicates that he knows all about the use of the wagons.'

'Not the smock, Watson, that was a coincidence. It had probably been used by his wife when she went blackberry picking. However, the fire disclosed a degree of intelligence that I would not have expected with Hedger'

One of the bushes alongside the level part of the line was searched and the Saxon gold plates and cups recovered. As for the thief he was awarded penal servitude for many years. Despite the efforts of his defence counsel, who argued most strongly that there was insufficient evidence to convict his client, it was a case of 'give a dog a bad name' because, as we were told, the accused had been in trouble with the law for a number of years.

Our last dinner at Uplea House was memorable for the delicious blackberry and apple pie.

THE END

THE ELECTRIFIED CANON

In which Sherlock Holmes becomes familiar with an electric gun capable of firing a projectile fifty miles. The gun has been developed by an electrifier, or magnetic engineer as he preferred to be called. He is killed and a key element of the gun is stolen. Sherlock Holmes is asked to track down the culprit and recover it before it falls into the wrong hands. The gun is an extremely dangerous weapon for those who are developing it and for anyone who eventually has to operate it. The intense energy developed by the series of powerful magnetic coils spaced along the barrel has proved difficult to restrain and direct

'This marmalade deserves greater recognition, Watson,' suggested my friend Holmes as he ate three pieces of conserve-laden toast with great relish.

'I have to admit, my dear fellow that I much prefer to watch you eat marmalade than have to breathe the air when you indulge in smoking that tobacco which I understand you call 'shag'.'

'Watson, I assumed you were not averse to the smoke from a pipe. I am certain it has therapeutic values not just for the smoker but also for those who are close by and can appreciate the pleasant aroma.'

One again I was not certain whether my friend was pulling my leg.

Our discussion on the competing merits of preserves, particularly marmalade, and the benefits of tobacco was interrupted by the arrival of two gentlemen. They introduced themselves as Admiral Anson and his secretary, Paymaster Lieutenant Haggard.

'Mr Holmes I have been advised to seek your help with finding the person who has killed a scientist engaged on secret work for the Admiralty, and who has stolen a piece of equipment vital to the success of the scientist's work.'

'What have your intelligence people or military intelligence discovered so far?'

'For a reason I cannot disclose to you, none of the intelligence departments in the Admiralty or at Horse Guards has been consulted.'

'I must say, Admiral, before you go any further, I am reluctant to take on a case when the client withholds information.'

'Mr Holmes, I can assure you that the reason is a good one. Until I can be certain of the facts I cannot say any more. We were also advised by an unnamed official in the government that the civil police and Scotland Yard in particular should not be involved. The fewer who know about the affair the better. Furthermore, I must have your assurance and that of Dr Watson that you will say nothing of what I am about to tell you.'

'As I presume that the navy's command of the seas is in danger of being compromised then I will listen to what you have come to tell me.'

'Thank you, Mr Holmes,' responded the admiral. 'About ten years ago Henry Campion, the scientist who has been killed, demonstrated at a Royal Society lecture a method of propelling an object along a track at high velocity using the power of electricity. He went on to develop models of carriages that could be propelled along railway lines. Apparently magnetic coils spaced along the track at intervals were energised in sequence by successive electrical charges. From the early experiments Campion went on to produce plans for a full size apparatus, but was unable to finance its construction. It was then that one of our more scientifically inclined officers in the Admiralty realised that the carriage could be replaced by a projectile, from which might be developed an electrified gun. Such a weapon might send an explosive charge over a distance of fifty or more miles. Campion was reluctant to consider an electrified gun, and we had to be most persuasive in convincing him that his reluctance was not in the interest of his country.'

'What persuaded him?'

'Money, Mr Holmes. Money, that great persuader. He realised that the funds allocated to him to proceed with the gun enabled him to develop in parallel a system for pacific applications; such as on the railways.'

'Admiral, an electrified gun is an astonishing idea, no wonder you do not want too many people to know of it,' said Holmes.

'Yes, if it works it will be a significant advance in gunnery. However, there is still much to be done. With the death of Campion the further research needed to perfect the weapon will be delayed.'

'You say more work needs to be done.'

'The experimental models have proved the concept. However, when a full size gun was built and tested it was discovered that some of the electrical energy was escaping and producing life-threatening charges for any one close by. Campion was killed just as he was about to install what he termed the 'key', a device that enabled the electrical energy to be better confined and controlled.'

'This key, Admiral Anson, is it just a normal key or something else?'

'It is in the shape of a baton. An ebony rod along which are spaced at intervals brass bands. The spacing varies so that it truly is a key to the successful control of the electrical charges. Only Campion knows, I mean knew, what the intervals have to be. Without the key the gun cannot be fired at its most powerful state. Of course, who ever took it must know that the key is of no use without the gun and the gun without the key.'

'Admiral, I cannot proceed with an investigation unless you are able to give me some indication of any person or persons who would want to seize the key. This brings me to the conclusion that who ever took it may have been intent on delaying progress with the perfection of the electrified gun. Would you have any one in mind? Perhaps a foreign power?'

'Before I reply to your question, Mr Holmes, I must again have your assurance and that of your companion, that what I am about to tell you must not be repeated or set down in writing.'

'Dr Watson and I have long been the trusted custodians of secrets on many occasions. You have our assurance that what you are about to tell us remains within our heads and no where else.'

'France, Mr Holmes.'

'France?'

'Surely, Sir, you are aware that both the navy and the army have to have contingency plans to combat political changes and threats emanating from countries across the Channel. For many years France has been considered as the principal potential threat. About two years ago we became aware that the French navy was perfecting a new class of torpedo boat able to attain a speed greater than any of our ships. These vessels have been gathered in the Channel ports such as Calais, Dieppe and Boulogne. They pose a threat, in the event of war, to our Channel Fleet. That is why the government has, in great secrecy, financed and supported with materiel, the electrified gun. Its range will allow us to bombard the French ports and make them untenable for their new torpedo boats.'

'Admiral, I am surprised at what you tell me. My understanding of the political climate of Europe is that in recent years our relationship with France has become far more amicable. Furthermore is not the increasing naval strength of Germany the greater threat?'

'That is correct, Mr Holmes. France is no longer treated as the only major threat. As for Germany, we are concerned over the way in which she is developing capital ships of a size and gun power to match ours. That is why we anticipate that Campion's gun, when developed even further, will reach as far as the new German naval harbours at the mouths of the Weser and the Elbe.'

'Are you saying that we are about to be involved in another war? We are not doing well in South Africa and the Kaiser's ministers advocate support for the Boers.'

'Not necessarily, Mr Holmes. What I mean to say is that in order to be prepared for a possible, not inevitable, conflict with France or Germany the navy must be ready at all times to respond to the demands of our political masters. Having a powerful gun able to reach a great distance is no different from having a proportion of our fleet cruising the Channel and the German Ocean with the gun crews fully prepared.'

'I assume that both the French and the German navies are fully aware that our plans are predicated on a future war?'

'Of that we can be certain. However, if it became known that we were developing a gun capable of reaching the French ports the diplomatic consequences could be such that Her Majesty's government would have to withdraw its support for the gun, in order not to disturb the present delicate rapport between us and France.'

'I see your problem, Admiral. You are concerned that who ever took the key is in the pay of either the French or the Germans. Campion was either killed trying to stop the theft of the key or his assailant killed him in order to delay the completion of the gun.'

'Could be either, Mr Holmes. Campion's body was only discovered earlier this morning, and it is a matter of great urgency. Now, will you take on the investigation?'

'Although I am reluctant to become involved with politics, nevertheless the affair promises to be a most intriguing one. Yes, I will take on the case.'

'I suggest you take the five twenty a.m. from Cannon Street tomorrow morning. You will arrive at Dover Priory at nine twenty five a.m.'

'Ah, the gun is at Dover.'

'Yes in HMS Placide a stone frigate a mile or two north of the harbour.'

At that I commented, 'Admiral, why is a ship of war there? The sea, surely, is to the south of Dover.'

'Dr Watson, a stone frigate is another name for a shore establishment. It so happens this one includes the remains of a Norman castle so that is an appropriate description.'

'Thank you, Admiral, I did wonder about the use of stone in place of iron and wood for Her Majesty's ships.'

Cannon Street station at five of a blustery November morning was not my idea of a venue for gentlemen. We had no difficulty in finding a compartment because, apart from a few workmen, we seemed to be the only people wanting to leave London at such an early hour. The locomotive at the head of our train gave the impression, from the desultory manner in which it started, that it found a still dark November morn not to its liking. Our progress was in fits and starts. We stopped at nearly every station and even at places where there was no station. At one station the driver of our train left the footplate and strolled back to the brakevan and joined the local stationmaster, some porters and others in a general discussion about the weather, racing certainties and local gossip. Only when they had concluded voicing their opinions did the driver regain his engine and, with no apparent urgency, start us on our way again.

At Dover Priory station we were met by the Paymaster Lieutenant and driven in a cab to HMS Placide. After a mile or two we could see the old Norman fortress and a number of more recent buildings that huddled close to the ancient walls. Most noticeable was the strange looking coils of wire set along the top of the wall in front of us that, I assumed, formed the perimeter of the establishment. 'That is a dangerous looking wire, Holmes,' I remarked.

'That, Watson,' he replied, 'is barbed wire. I saw some when I was in America. It is a most effective way of keeping animals and humans out or, alternatively, keeping them in. It is also sometimes the cause of the range wars, in which cattlemen dispute the ownership of land, or resent the way in which shepherds fence off thousands of acres and so prevent the cattlemen's herds roaming freely across the prairies.'

Once through the gate with its armed sentries we were taken to the Admiral's quarters. 'Good morning gentlemen,' said he. 'I much appreciate your willingness to suffer the rigours of a train journey so early in the day. As soon as you have refreshed yourselves and had some breakfast we will go to where Campion was killed. Everything has been left exactly as it was discovered yesterday.'

The admiral conducted us to where the scientist's rooms were. We passed through a heavy oak door that led into a lobby at the end of which was another heavy door standing open. Lying just behind it was the body of Campion. He was on his side. The lamp, that he must have been holding, lay shattered on the carpet. Another lamp, still burning, stood on top of a small safe, the door of which was open.

I examined the victim's skull and it was clear that he had suffered a severe blow that had fractured his skull.

'What do you make of the injury, Watson?' asked Holmes.

'Without doubt he was struck with a heavy weapon, possibly metal, the end of which had about five or six knobs or projections,' was my answer.

'We did not find anything like that,' responded the Admiral. 'As we were advised by the unnamed person in some government department, we left everything as we found it on discovering the body, even the burning lamp.' Holmes looked at me and his lips formed the name 'Mycroft'.

Holmes started his customary scrutiny of the scene of a crime. I took the opportunity to improve my detective skill by studying the room and its contents. The stone walls were devoid of decoration, hangings or pictures. The large desk and numerous shelves and cupboards took up most of the room. When I stooped and looked into the safe I saw that its contents had not been disturbed. All the paper folders, bound papers and books were still arranged in an orderly manner. Who ever had struck down Campion had had no need to search for the key to the gun. It must have been in full view on one of the shelves. I also observed that the lamp which was on top of the safe and still burning was of an unusual type and therefore markedly different from the one that Campion had been holding. I thought, 'why two different lamps, one of which was not of a type usually found in a house. Presumably, it could have been carried by the murderer.'

I did not consider it significant that the heavy oak door stood open because a number of people must have come in and gone out. In the lobby there were more books and papers on shelves and on a small desk. Some of the books were lying open and there were a few papers spread on the desk. Exercising what little detective skill I had acquired at the side of the country's foremost scientific detective, I deduced that Campion had been working in the lobby on some papers or seeking information from one of the books and then he had come into the main room to take something out of the safe. As he stooped to open the safe he was struck a lethal blow.

My thoughts were interrupted by Holmes inquiring about the weather the previous evening. 'I read in this morning's paper, which I bought at the Priory station, that a full gale was blowing, the noise of which would have prevented anyone hearing any untoward sounds from the rooms'

'It was a force eight gale, Mr Holmes. It was even stronger here on top of the hill,' replied the Admiral. 'It was difficult to walk about or hear much over the screaming wind. We could have been at sea.'

'Admiral,' said Holmes, 'the idea of an electric gun intrigues me. Presumably there is no powder charge needed?'

'None at all. Apart from some intense flashes of electrical discharges the gun has the advantage, in addition to its great range, of not revealing its position to an enemy. That is, of course, as long as it is not fired at night.' responded the admiral. 'There is to be a test firing tomorrow. Perhaps you and Dr Watson would like to be witnesses. Although the essential key is missing an earlier version can be used that will enable the gun to achieve a range of ten miles.'

We retired for a rather disturbed, noisy night of gusting winds; our quarters were individual rooms within the 'stone ship'. The next morning we were taken to a disused water reservoir hidden in a clump of trees. Looking down into the deep circular concrete-lined tank we could see the many steel rods and beams that made up a structure that rose from the bottom of the reservoir near where we were standing. To one side and partly hidden by the trees was an astonishing sight. Many large sheets of some metallic substance hung from wires fastened to the trees. There were about fifty the area of each was about that of a tennis court. The strange structure was surrounded by a barbed wire fence.

The admiral pointed down into the pit. 'That is the electric gun. The series of copper coils you can see along its length is what sends a projectile at great velocity. At present it is aligned to point out over the channel. The steam engine you can hear is driving a dynamo to charge up the array of large metal plates hanging in the trees over there so that they store electricity at a great potential.'

'Admiral, what of any vessel in the Channel at this moment. Will it not be in danger?' asked Holmes.

'Indeed it would. However, I have just listened to the telephonic apparatus that is joined to a similar apparatus on the top of Dover Castle where one of the crew keeps watch for any ships that might be sailing into danger. He has just signalled that the range is clear.'

Two lieutenants were busy making final adjustments. Thick cables were being joined to the base of the gun. One shouted up to us. 'Fully charged Sir, ready to fire.' They both moved into a metal cage.

The admiral signalled with his hand and the pit became an inferno of electrical discharges as if a fierce thunderstorm had been trapped within its depth. I could see the two officers inside the metal cage over whose surface electrical discharges flowed.

'What an amazing sight,' I exclaimed. 'Are those two all right? They are surrounded by electrical fire.'

'They are inside a Faraday cage, Dr Watson. As long as they keep within it they can come to no harm,' replied the admiral.

Then came a blinding flash that seemed to travel along the framework that pointed upward. A few seconds after came a strange rumbling or rather a booming sound, as if a cannon had been fired some way off. 'We always hear that sound after we have fired a projectile. No one appears to know why,' said the admiral.

After that remarkable demonstration of the power of electricity we repaired to the admiral's cabin. During the ensuing discussion Holmes asked, 'Admiral, apart from yourself and your secretary, who else knows how the electric gun works?'

'Only two. They are the lieutenants Fresnal and Gordon you saw operating the gun.'

'But what of the men who make the parts and assemble the gun. They, surely, must be aware of its purpose.'

'Of course they know it is a gun but are not aware of how it works. They have little or no idea about the manner in which the electrical charges are provided and controlled. They tend to be rather careless and sadly one of them was killed when a charge of electricity escaped its bounds and attacked him. He was standing too close when Campion was conducting some tests. Above all they, and everyone working on the gun, are aware that under no circumstances must they reveal to any one outside the establishment the workings and purpose of the gun. Were they to do so they would be faced with imprisonment in solitary confinement for an indefinite time.'

'Therefore, the two lieutenants we saw have to be suspects.'

'Surely not!' exclaimed the admiral. 'I selected them myself from the top ten gunnery pupils at Whale Island. As Lieutenant Gordon went ashore immediately after breakfast he could not have been involved. That leaves Fresnal.'

'Therefore for the time being we have to concentrate on Fresnal,' Holmes replied. 'The principal problem facing us is what was the motive for the killing and the theft? What could be the object of stealing the key? As a length of ebony rod with some copper bands it is, presumably, on its own, of little value. We also have to consider whether the killing of Campion was premeditated or the result of a sudden rage? The facts suggest that Campion had been struck on the head by his attacker wielding a heavy, studded object. Whether the door of the safe was open or closed at the time or had been opened by his assailant, is a difficult question to answer.'

During a subsequent discussion of the case with the admiral, Holmes reported on what he had found when he had made a meticulous inspection of the room. 'I found these three objects that might indicate who the killer had been. One is this short length of dark blue coloured wool, another this Vespa match that had failed to light and, the third, this crumb of cake. The validity of these clues depended on the fact that, as you told me Admiral, the carpet in the room had been taken up and removed outside and beaten the previous morning. Furthermore I understand Campion had not left the room or the lobby after the carpet had been replaced and had not eaten any cake. Lieutenant Fresnal, however, had eaten cake in the wardroom

234

about thirty minutes before the assumed time of the killing. The gangway log shows that two hours before he had gone ashore, as you say, to the house he rents in the nearby village. I regret to say this but I need to visit Fresnal's house without him knowing who I am. There may be something there which will either confirm our suspicions or completely exonerate the lieutenant.'

'An interesting exercise, Mr Holmes,' commented the Admiral. 'Nevertheless I cannot say I entirely approve of such methods to gain information.'

'I really have no alternative,' replied Holmes. 'Now, there is something else that I found in Campion's rooms. It is this copy of an old newspaper. As you can see, a parliamentary report had been circled by an inked line. It tells of the heated arguments in the House during the naval and military departments' estimates. A member who supported the navy's need for more funds rebutted an army member's claim that the navy was taking a far greater share of the available funds. Another report that caught my eye is in this cutting from the Morning Post that informed its readers about an unseemly argument, expressed loudly, in the Army and Navy club. A general and an admiral exchanged verbal blows over the development of a new type of gun. The general opined that such a weapon was in the remit of the army's coast defence batteries. The admiral considered that large coastal artillery pieces could be better deployed by the navy.

'Yes, I was aware of the exchanges. I consider the behaviour of those officers to be beyond the pale,' responded the admiral.

'It seems to me, Admiral that the two departments tend to put prestige before that of the good defence of the realm. I read that the subject of coastal defence artillery was a particularly contentious issue. Reluctantly I come to the opinion that there are some admirals and generals who would put the advancement of their careers above that of their duty.'

'Mr Holmes, what an astonishing thing to say.'

'Astonishing or not it could explain who is behind the attempt to steal the key and plans of the electric gun. The navy is developing a gun that the army considers should be with them. Unprofessional skulduggery within these shores could be the answer and not agents acting on behalf of a foreign country, such as France.'

'Mr Holmes what a preposterous idea,' exclaimed the admiral with barely concealed rage. 'But, surely, they would not kill to achieve their purpose?'

'I admit that would not be expected, however desirable the outcome.'

Later in the day Holmes returned from his visit to Fresnal's house. He recounted to the admiral and myself what had happened.

'I personated an official from the county authorities who was surveying property in the area. I was able to convince the servant who answered the door bell to allow me access to the hallway of the house while she went to inform Fresnal's wife. That gave me the opportunity to see into the adjacent rooms and observe a number of significant items. I could see that the furniture, hangings and ornaments were of high quality and expensive. The household was far more lavish than one might have expected on the pay of a lieutenant. That conclusion suggests that if he were the killer money was not the object.

At tea in the wardroom, of which we had become honorary members, the officers, as was customary did not discuss naval affairs. However, one did exclaim, 'I say, the French are getting rather touchy. They complain that, without any warning, we are lobbing shells into the Channel.' None of the others round the table responded other than to grunt to indicate they had heard but obviously considered such a subject was not one that a gentleman should raise at table. We made no comment because we were aware that only one or two of those present knew about the electrical gun.

After tea Holmes interrupted my attempt to understand, from an article in the Morning Post, why the government was so anxious to placate the French over some incident that had occurred on the border between one of our colonies and one of theirs. In my opinion the French did not even deserve to have colonies; particularly as they had marched into them and made claim to them irrespective of the will of the inhabitants.

As we discussed the article Fresnal passed by. After he had gone Holmes said, 'Watson, apart from what I learned about his family there is something strange about Fresnal. He has a furtive manner and keeps moving from one place to another as if looking for something. Furthermore, I observed in his house a long knitted scarf the colour of which matched the piece of wool I found in Campion's room.'

'Oh, surely, he is just a rather active man. The responsibility for the firing of the gun must impose a great mental strain on him.'

'Ah, look, he is making for the gun. He is either going to make some adjustment of the apparatus preparatory to tomorrow's test or for some other reason. As the admiral told us, the gun and its surroundings can be a very dangerous place and that no one is permitted to enter the gun pit on their own. It can be even more dangerous at night. Despite the abundance of electricity down in the pit the only illumination is that provided by oil lamps or candles. We must follow him.'

'Oh, come on, my dear fellow, he is a naval officer albeit he is not at sea. Even though he is under suspicion, he is perfectly within his rights to go about his duties.'

'Remember, Watson, the admiral told us that the metal curtains hanging among the trees are fully charged with electricity in preparation for the next firing. To go alone into the pit would be extremely dangerous. Fresnal is up to something and I do not believe it is for the good.'

'You are guessing.'

'I do not guess. A premonition, not a guess.'

Realising that argument would not dissuade my friend we set off for the gun emplacement and, with some hesitation, I followed him down the steep staircase that led to the bottom of the pit. The only light came from a lantern that Fresnal had taken down with him. We stood there surrounded by the strange arrangement of metal rods and thick snake-like cables that were supported on what appeared to be large upended domestic clay flower pots. We could not see Fresnal. His lantern stood on the ground. Our silent contemplation of the scene and what our next step had to be was interrupted.

'Raise your hands. One wrong move and I will have to shoot both of you as spies.'

His voice came out of the darkness among the machinery of the gun. 'Move into the metal cage on your right and stay there until I decide what to do with you. Make no unnecessary move because I will not hesitate to shoot. I can see you but you cannot see me. Once I have made some connections I'll join you.'

'Fresnal are you going to fire the gun and if so why?' asked Holmes.

'I am, now that I have the vital key for maximum range.'

'If you do, where will the projectile land?'

'Close to Dieppe,' came the reply.

'People will be killed.'

'An unfortunate consequence of a plan whose purpose is of far greater importance than the lives of a few hundred citizens of France. You are attempting to interfere, and delay what I have always intended to do at the first opportunity. It is probable that the attack on France will be responded to immediately. The fleet of torpedo boats in Boulogne and Dieppe will descend on the Channel Fleet and sink every ship. Enough of this useless talk I am about to launch the first projectile. Of course, I may die in the attempt because the gun has never been fired at the full electrical charge. I will not regret it if you are killed with me.'

'All I can say is that you have grossly underestimated the readiness and strength of our ships.'

'And, you, Mr Holmes, overestimate your ability to escape from a predicament, such as the one in which you now find yourself. Your companion has grossly exaggerated it in his records of your adventures.'

Suddenly there were blinding flashes of light as Fresnal started to make some adjustments to the terrifying apparatus. As calmly as I could I whispered, 'Holmes, did you bring your gun?'

'No, I assumed you would have yours.'

'I saw no need as we were to visit a naval establishment.'

'Then we have only one chance to save ourselves.'

The electrical discharges increased in number and intensity. 'So this is what it would be like to be up in the clouds in the middle of a violent thunderstorm,' was all I could think about.

I felt rather than saw Holmes make a sudden move forward, followed by a scream from Fresnal and an even greater number of flashes started. Holmes dived back into the Faraday cage. The pit was filled with electrical discharges shooting from one side to the other. In their glare we watched in horror as Fresnal became a heap of carbon. He must have stumbled and in reaching forward to steady himself touched a lethal part of the apparatus.

When the electricity had spent itself the admiral and others came down to us and led us back out of the pit.

'What did you do to stop him?' I asked Holmes, as we climbed the stairs away from that dreadful sight.

'I used my sword stick. I was able to hurl it as if it were a javelin. It did the trick.' said Holmes, though I was still unsure of his meaning.

Once we were back in the admiral's cabin Holmes was handed a letter. He read it. 'This is an astounding revelation,' he exclaimed. 'It comes from Mycroft. Apparently Fresnal was an agent of a foreign power. He was born in France but from the age of four was raised by an English family. They were unaware that he had been persuaded to become involved in espionage. He had been carefully groomed by his masters for his role. By some means or other they ensured that he succeeded in the entrance examination for the Royal Navy and graduated as a midshipman. He was then implanted within the Navy awaiting a summons to undertake espionage tasks. The plan intended that Britain would be forced to sue for peace and, in doing so, lose its command of the seas and, no doubt, hand over some of our territories. The Royal Navy would be weakened to such an extent that other actions could be taken against Britain so that we would never again be a major power in the world.'

'Mr Holmes, you have yet to tell me how Fresnal killed Campion,' asked the admiral.

'He did not. His is a case of accidental death.'

'Surely not!'

'Recall the arrangement of the scientist's two rooms. There is the outer door and then an inner door to the room where the safe was. Fresnal certainly was intent on securing the key. He opened the outer door. As he did so a strong gust of wind rushed in and slammed the inner door against the side of Campion's head. Hence the unusual injury which you observed. The heavy wrought iron door handle was the assassin. Fresnal, on finding Campion prostrate and the safe door open, realised that chance had placed the key in his hands.

I doubt that he even stopped to see if the scientist was alive or dead.'

I was pleased that we could leave the bare walls and bleakness of the inappropriately named HMS Placide and return to 221B Baker Street. As the train took us toward London I thought about our adventure and the peril into which we had been led. Among a number of questions I put to my companion was, 'Holmes, did you come to that conclusion about the door knob when we were examining the room?'

'No. I only decided that that had to be the answer when I spent most of the night pondering all aspects of the case. Somewhere around three in the morning the door of the room, I should say cabin, next to mine was violently slammed. That set me thinking and I recalled that you bent forward alongside the open door to examine the contents of the safe. I then remembered that your head had been level with the door handle.'

'An important conclusion,' said I.

'Now this time, my dear Watson, do not even think of writing up what has happened as another adventure. The subject is far too delicate and we gave our word not reveal anything we heard or saw. Think of the diplomatic consequences were it to be known that one of our guns was not only capable of reaching across the Channel but might have been actually fired and a projectile landed in France.'

'In the confusion of those terrible moments in the cage I did not see clearly how you saved us.'

'Simple, dear chap, I hurled my stick at Fresnal and more by chance than intent it struck him and the apparatus at the same time, so joining him in the lethal electrical outpourings.'

'What a story to tell!' I thought. 'Perhaps, in years to come I may be able to recount how Holmes and I had come closer to death than in any of our other adventures.'

THE END

Also from MX Publishing

MX Publishing is the world's largest specialist Sherlock Holmes publisher, with over a hundred titles and fifty authors creating the latest in Sherlock Holmes fiction and non-fiction.

From traditional short stories and novels to travel guides and quiz books, MX Publishing cater for all Holmes fans.

The collection includes leading titles such as *Benedict Cumberbatch In Transition* and *The Norwood Author* which won the 2011 Howlett Award (Sherlock Holmes Book of the Year).

MX Publishing also has one of the largest communities of Holmes fans on Facebook with regular contributions from dozens of authors.

www.mxpublishing.com

Also from MX Publishing

Sherlock Holmes Short Story Collections

Sherlock Holmes and the Murder at the Savoy

Sherlock Holmes and the Skull of Kohada Koheiji

Look out for the new novel from Mike Hogan
– *The Scottish Question.*

www.mxpublishing.com

245

Also from MX Publishing

Our bestselling short story collections 'Lost Stories of Sherlock Holmes', 'The Outstanding Mysteries of Sherlock Holmes', 'Untold Adventures of Sherlock Holmes' (and the sequel 'Studies in Legacy') and 'Sherlock Holmes in Pursuit'.

Links

MX Publishing are proud to support the Save Undershaw campaign – the campaign to save and restore Sir Arthur Conan Doyle's former home. Undershaw is where he brought Sherlock Holmes back to life, and should be preserved for future generations of Holmes fans.

Save Undershaw   www.facebook.com/saveundershaw

Sherlockology   www.sherlockology.com

MX Publishing   www.mxpublishing.com

You can read more about Sir Arthur Conan Doyle and Undershaw in Alistair Duncan's book (share of royalties to the Undershaw Preservation Trust) – *An Entirely New Country* and in the amazing compilation Sherlock's Home – The Empty House (all royalties to the Trust).